A Novel By

Makenz

Xpress Yourself Publishing, LLC

Xpress Yourself Publishing, LLC
P.O. Box 1615
Upper Marlboro, MD 20773

www.xpressyourselfpublishing.org

For information about special discounts for bulk purchases,
please contact Xpress Yourself Publishing Special Sales:
Phone: 301-404-5615 — Fax: 1-530-685-5346
info@xpressyourselfpublishing.org.

Manufacturered in the United States of America

ISBN-10: 0-9722990-7-6
ISBN-13: 978-0-9722990-7-7

Distribution by:
Baker & Taylor and Ingram Book Group

Interior and Cover Designed by:
The Writer's Assistant
www.thewritersassistant.com

Also by Makenzi

That's How I Like It!

Acknowledgments

    This whole experience would not have happen without my love, commitment and faith in God. You showed me a vision and I followed; no questions asked. Thank you for instilling in me the POWER and STRENGTH to believe.

    My parents, Hiram and Vernell…together, you both taught me many life lessons. Thank you for loving each other and showing me how to live and love. Daddy, you raised a spoiled brat. You are a special man and I want to thank you for all of your support and true love.

    Mommy, (RIP 3/2004), I miss calling you up on the phone just to hear you fuss. I can picture your smile, hear your voice, and see your face. Oh, what a beautiful face! Even though you're not here in the flesh, you are here in spirit. Thank you for pushing me to live life to the fullest. When I was a young girl, I did not understand things you told me, but now that I am a woman, I understand completely. Love you, sunshine!!!!

    Shelly, you are such a wonderful sister. You would say as a child I would get on your nerves, but now you can't go a day without talking with me. You were one of my first true dedicated fans and supporters of this journey. I love you.

    Sharmaine and Jasmine…Auntie loves you with everything I have. I am so proud of the both of you. Remember, you have the resources to succeed in this crazy world.

Frank, do you regret marrying into this family yet? I know we are a handful, but I have to admit I would not have picked a better brother-in-law.

Sashelle, we have a lot to be proud of despite all we have experienced. You are a real drill sergeant; I went through boot camp the whole time I was writing this book because you were on me every single day. Thank you for the countless hours you put in at the computer, spicing up and creating chapters. Nevertheless, it paid off. You know I admire you for everything you stand for. You are a great cousin and friend, and anybody would be silly not to have you in their life. "Go on brush your shoulders off"!!!!

Vanessa, I am glad we were able to build a friendship. You are a faithful friend and I'm glad I can count on you for anything. You are about business, and I need that in my life. Thanks! Love Ya!

Geri, I don't know anyone who keeps up so much sh**. You are the one cousin who keeps me on my toes. You always have a plan and plot in place. Thanks for the encouraging words and the open heart and mind. I love you!

Thanks to my editor, Carla Dean of U Can Mark My Word. Thanks, girl. I appreciate you.

Thanks to my family and friends for your support. You have supported me in many different stages of my life, and I appreciate and love you all. I did not know this would be such a hard task. Now I know!

Finally, yet most importantly, thank you, VYSS. You ladies never gave up, and for that I'm grateful. We have arrived. Remember the motto: ***"To promote, stimulate, and motivate the creativity and vision of African American females."***

MAKENZI

Dangerously

A Novel By

Makenzi

Chapter 1

Christian

The pleasures of life. Yeah right!!! Not for me. Ain't shit pleasurable about the life I'm living, which only leaves me with the choice of deciding which will be more painful…the pain I will endure if I choose to continue living or the pain I may experience upon death. Which is worst? Decisions, decisions.

Should I take a bullet to the head, pump my body full of prescription drugs, lie down and never wake up, or slit my wrists and allow the life to slowly seep from my body? Or is it God's will for me to stay and endure all this pain? Decisions, decisions.

Dear God,

I really don't know where to start because I haven't been the most faithful, praying person lately. See, I guess I never really felt I had a real reason to pray. For the most part, everything had been going pretty much the way I thought it was supposed to.

My daddy provided everything for me to make up for the absentee mother who birthed me. Although, it's probably Daddy's fault my mom didn't stay around in the first place. The reason I say this is because he was and still is a womanizer. He messed around on her numerous times and yet she kept finding it in her heart to forgive him. That is, until she came home that fateful day and listened to the answering machine as Aunt Whitney fussed about someone coming to pick me up since she had to go to work and I'd been at her house all day. My trifling daddy had dropped me off so he could run be with Delores, his ex. By this point, my mom had taken all she could endure. She left that same day, with me still at Aunt Whit's, and *never* returned.

I was very young when my mother left, so I don't remember much about her. I do have pictures of her that I look at often, attempting to imagine what she would look in this present time. I can honestly say I am the spitting image of her and have been told this from relatives and close friends of the family more times than I can count. Sometimes when I look at her pictures, I have to do a double take, almost mistaking them for pictures of myself.

From the look of the photos, she appears to be the same height I am, about five foot one, and we're both on the petite side. In this one picture in particular, she has a medium-length feather hairstyle, but I can tell her hair is thick, just like mine. I often daydream about the closeness we would share if she sat in my salon chair and allowed me to work my magic on her hair. Afterwards, she would leave…proud of her daughter's talent, even though I disappointed her by dropping out of college

She has almond-shaped eyes, same as I do, except her eyes are a lighter brown than mine. Her hair is a bit sandier, also. I dye mine because of my dislike for brown hair. We both have pudgy noses and very thin lips. I have one dimple; she has two. I also have her to thank for my bushy-ass eyebrows. The only difference is I get mine waxed. I guess the picture was taken before waxing became popular.

In the photo, she is wearing something that resembles a one-piece purple jogging outfit, which I must admit is somewhat stylish. It was fitting her well, and yes, my mom has, or should I say had, a shape. I don't know what she has *now*. She's very cute and looks to be about eighteen, but there's no date on the picture, so I can't really be sure.

Oh, how I wish I could remember more about her. What I know of her are the basics. For instance, I know her name is Carmen and that she's originally from DC. She met Daddy when he was there visiting some friends who were in medical school at Howard University. Daddy kept returning to the DC area so he could "run into her". Finally, giving into his persistence, she agreed to date him and, from what I am told by Aunt Whit, got pregnant almost immediately. With Daddy not ready to be neither a father nor a husband, he abandoned her in DC and left no information on how he could be contacted. I still don't want to believe my father, whom I adore with every bone in my body, could actually be that coldhearted toward someone, let alone the woman who was carrying his child.

Aunt Whit said that somehow my mom found out Dad's phone number and kept calling and begging him to come back so they could be a family, but he didn't want anything to do with her or her unborn child, especially since he had moved on and had plans of marrying Delores. Well, his decision didn't flying well with Carmen's dad, my grandfather, who was a sergeant in the U.S. Marines and hunted Daddy's ass down. My mom's family was successful in getting in contact with Aunt Whit, since it was Dad's last known address. After talking to my grandfather, Aunt Whit was on the next bus to DC.

Supposedly, Aunt Whit called Daddy and cursed him out about leaving Carmen pregnant and alone. She told Daddy to get his shit together and meet her in DC that night or else she was going to call Delores and tell all. Needless to say, Daddy didn't arrive in time, and Aunt Whit, who was there for my birth, got her gossipin' tail on the phone and spilled the beans to Delores. After hearing what Aunt Whit had to say, Delores no longer wanted anything to do with Daddy…at least that's what she said at the time. By the time Daddy made it to DC, their engagement was off.

Upon learning this, my grandfather put together a "short notice" wedding for Daddy and Carmen at the chapel on the base. Aunt Whit said there were about fifty people in attendance and that it actually turned out nice. After the ceremony, a small dinner reception was held at a restaurant on the base. The next day, Daddy, Carmen, Aunt Whit, and I left DC and headed home.

Once back home, it didn't take long for Delores to fall for Daddy's tricks again. Daddy started fucking around with Delores again right after speaking his vows at his shotgun marriage. He ran her some bullshit of how I was a mistake and that I might not even be his, but since he was an *'honorable'* man, he had to do the right thing. Daddy did have one thing right, and that is, I didn't look like him. If Carmen got pregnant as quickly as they said, then I guess he was right to feel like I could've been another man's child.

I think he did grow to love my mother, though. I believe after a while he started to realize she didn't try to "trap" him, and that they both just got caught up.

Aunt Whit said my mother was a very good wife. Although she proved to be such, he wouldn't allow her to do things outside of the home, like work or hang out with her newfound friends. On top of that, she was only permitted to go home twice a year. It's still hard for me to imagine Mel Johnson, *my daddy*, controlling some damn body. But it's true. And because of his controlling ways and infidelity, my mom walked right out on *both* of our asses and *NEVER* came back.

I think this is why I tried desperately to hold on to Kory, my husband. I just couldn't take the thought of being out here in this world alone. Hell, I grew up lonely. Why would I want to live my adult life the same exact way?

I know you're asking why I'm praying to you now seeing as I haven't prayed since the incident with Kory in the shop.

Well, I am going to be honest with you, God. I stopped believing in you.

I mean, why would you take my mother and leave me to be raised alone by my doggish, philandering daddy? Sure, many women were in and out of our life, but none could take the place of my mother. I gave nothing but attitude to every woman he became involved with, especially that bitch Delores. I sent her ass steppin' as soon as I could turn my lips up to say the words. Imagine that…me, Christian Alicia Johnson-Banks, giving someone hell.

Anyway, after praying faithfully each night and going to church with Aunt Whitney every Sunday morning, I decided prayer didn't work since my mom never returned. Therefore, I stopped praying. I mean, here I am a little girl and my mother just up and abandoned me because of some stuff my father did. I could see her leaving him, *but me?* She could've at least taken me with her. She shouldn't have left me behind like that. *You* shouldn't have allowed that. That's why I stopped praying. But when I felt in danger that day with Kory whilin' out on me over some jealous issues he was dealing with pertaining to my previous relationship with Doug, whom I had dated prior to marrying Kory, I stopped and prayed. And because you spared my life that night, God, I am praying to you again.

I joined church with Aunt Whit when I was six years old. I was baptized, attended Sunday School and Vacation Bible School, and was even on the Junior Usher Board for a while. I assume that from all of my involvement in the church I'm saved, and therefore believe there's a part of me that still has remaining faith in you, which I suppose is the reason why I am writing you this letter now.

What I actually want to know is this, and I'll get to the point, God. I have been reading the Bible all day. Hard to believe, huh? Yes, me, Christian Alicia Johnson-Banks, reading the Bible. But I didn't know where else to turn to find the answers to my questions about suicide.

You see, Dear God, I am ready to go. I can't take this anymore. I hate my life. I hate living. It's a chore for me just to wake up in the morning. I've thought this decision through carefully, but haven't decided on the way in which I will take my own life…shoot myself, overdose, or slit my wrists. None of these options are appealing to me, but I feel as though I have no other choice. I know I should consider the affects my demise will have on Kory and Kamryn, our daughter, but from the looks of it, I am not of any use to them in my current state of mind while living. It's a constant mental battle…one of which I am slowly losing.

Which brings me to my pressing question: If I go through with this, can you show some mercy and allow me to enter the gates of heaven? I do NOT want to go to hell.

Speaking of death, Aunt Whit told me about four years ago that she heard through the grapevine that my mom had died and was buried somewhere out west. She could be right about this, because according to Daddy, Carmen lived dangerously her entire life. I never even looked up the death record to see if in fact my mother had died. I felt as long as I didn't know for sure there would always be a chance Aunt

Whit didn't know what the hell she was talking about. I still want to believe the woman who gave birth to me, Carmen Jean Johnson, will one day return and make everything all right.

To this very day, Aunt Whit isn't speaking to me because I treated her so badly when she delivered the news to me. I mean, how in the fuck, *(pardon my language, God)*, are you supposed to react when someone calls you at work and says, "Baby, your good-for-nothin' mama done died on them streets in California"?

Died on the streets? What is that supposed to mean, God? Carmen was from DC, so what was she doing out in California? If my grandfather used his rank to find Daddy way back when, why didn't he use it to find Carmen? There are so many things that absolutely make no sense at all to me…especially the fact that Carmen Jean Johnson supposedly died on the streets in California and the only person who heard about it was Whitney Johnson.

Aunt Whit's deliverance didn't sit well with me and I let her know it, along with a few other choice words. She hasn't spoken directly to me since, but Daddy said she did send me a card to the house to say how sorry she was. Fuck Whit! And if I could have it my way and die tonight, like I pray I do, we won't speak again until she gets to wherever it is we go when we die.

But right now, I am not thinking about Whit or anyone else. All I know is that I'm in pain and I can't take this anymore. So as I lay here in my pajamas, so damn funky from me not getting out of the bed for the last three days, I beg you, Dear Lord, to hear my prayer: If my mom is up there in heaven with you, I want to give her one more chance to come get me and take me home with her. Amen.

Chapter 2

Marcella

A year ago, Lance and I began our counseling sessions, and ever since, I have had a newfound respect for the psychiatric profession. Psychiatrists can make a person expose their innermost secrets and provide a solution to any problem. For the past year, Lance has been pouring his heart out to this lady. I found out things about him I never knew and probably never would have known if it weren't for his infidelity and our agreement to attend these sessions.

From the day when I caught Lance in a sexual act with a man, I never thought our marriage would last another minute. The mere sight of him made me nauseous. Lance confessed at first it was curiosity, and then from curiosity came the enjoyment of having sex with men. Now, one year later, and after considerable progress with our weekly sessions, I couldn't be happier, except for the fact that I also discovered not only was Lance sleeping with men, but he'd had an affair with a girl named Rosalita, a young Puerto Rican bank teller from the hood.

As if the revelation of the affair wasn't enough, I learned Lance fathered a child with this woman, a five-year-old daughter named Selena, with whom he has had a relationship with since her birth. He and Rosalita had an arrangement going on until Lance confessed to me about Selena.

Lance told me that Rosalita had threatened hundreds of times to call and tell me about their affair and the baby. She would only use this form of blackmail when she wanted more money from Lance. However, the shit had to stop when Alexis, our daughter, was born. Lance was paying out too much money each month and it was draining him financially to keep his illegitimate child undercover. I'm glad Lance told me at the counselor's, because if it had been at any other time, I may have put his black ass out of the house.

When I found out about Selena, I had second thoughts about working on my marriage. Yeah, my husband was a cheater with people of both sexes and I did forgive him, or else I wouldn't have agreed to go to counseling with him. However, when it came time to welcome the new addition to our family, someone who would be a permanent part of our lives, I had to re-think my commitment to this marriage. It was bad enough I had to accept the fact that he already had a son by the name of Casey. However, it was much easier to deal with since he'd fathered Casey with a woman named Joyce before we were married, and also because Casey didn't visit much. It was almost as if he didn't exist, except for the hefty monthly child support that was a constant reminder to us that he *did* in fact exist.

After weeks of his begging, I finally let Lance bring Selena over to the house to meet me. Can you believe Rosalita's ass wanted to come over, too? She couldn't be serious! Did she really think I would allow the woman who had an affair with my husband inside of my home? I don't think so.

At first, I was a little nervous about meeting Selena. I didn't know how she would react to me and what her mother had been telling her about me. However, as soon as she walked into the house, she ran over and gave me a hug, relieving some of the anxiety I was experiencing. When I looked at her, I saw an innocent little girl with big almond-shaped eyes, long eyelashes, deep dimples, braids in her hair, and petite hands and feet. She looked a lot like Lance, but I could tell right away that she was mixed because of her jet black hair and olive complexion.

I had to admire the outfit she was wearing, a sundress in my favorite colors of pink and green, pink sandals, sun hat, and even a purse to match. Selena pulled out some candy from her purse and offered me a piece. The next thing she asked me brought tears to my eyes. She asked if she should call me Mommy II or Marcella. I told her it was okay to call me Marcella. Selena was talking so fast, I could barely understand what she was saying. I did understand her when she asked if she could meet her baby sister, Alexis. She said Lance had told her all about Alexis and that she was excited about meeting her. To her disappointment, Alexis had gone with her aunt Christian and cousin Kamryn earlier that day and wouldn't be back until later in the evening.

After Lance departed to go open the club, I prepared lunch for Selena and me. While eating a meal consisting of chicken nuggets, French fries, and fruit punch, we sat and talked about school, Alexis, her friends, and her favorite TV show, SpongeBob SquarePants. After the long talk and laughs, we sat and colored pictures, and afterwards, I read her a story and she read me one, also. I could tell she was a very smart girl. Not once did Selena talk about her mother or any member of her family the whole time she was at our house that day. I hate that I had to meet Selena under these circumstances. She was a sweet child and I prayed I wouldn't end up holding any resentment toward her because of her being the product of my husband's infidelity.

Upon Alexis' return home, she ran to give me a hug, then noticed Selena sitting on the floor and questioned who she was. I introduced Alexis to her big sister, Selena. To my surprise, they hit it off instantly, and Alexis excitedly pulled Selena to her room to show her all of her toys, where they stayed and played for several hours.

When Lance called to check-in, I was excited to tell him all about the day Selena and I had, and how smooth everything was going between the children. Lance expressed his appreciation for my patience and the effort I was giving to accept Selena not only into our home, but also into our lives. Before returning home, Lance made a stop by our local Blockbusters so we could enjoy movies with the children. He did well with his selections, choosing *Cinderella*, the version starring Brandy, and every little girl's favorite, *Pocahontas*. Just like at the movies, we had the set-up of popcorn, Raisinets, juice, and Twizzlers. I even laid out a blanket for Selena and Alexis to lie on. From the expression on her face, it was clear to see that Selena was having the time of her life. By the middle of the second movie, both of the crumb snatchers were knocked out sleep on the floor.

After putting them to bed, with Lance scooping up Selena and me carrying Alexis, I headed for the shower, exhausted from the long day I had. After adjusting the water settings, I allowed the steam to envelope my body as I removed my clothing. Assuming that I was alone, I was slightly startled when Lance walked up behind me and started kissing on the back of my neck, which he knew was one of my spots. Lance said that since I had been a good girl he was going to give me a treat for my good deeds. What would have been a real treat is if the sex would have gotten better over the years, but it hadn't.

The next thing I knew, Lance had me bent over the bathtub and was fucking the shit out of me (or so he thought) from behind with his little ass dick. Lance thought I was screaming and getting pleasure from his short, sporadic thrusts, but truth is I was really laughing and losing my fucking mind. If the survival of my marriage to this man was based purely on his sexual performance, it would have been over a long time ago. Caught up in the humor of the situation, I forgot the shower was running until I felt the temperature change of the water, which was hitting my back and which was also the only thing giving me pleasure at that moment. With me still bent over, with one hand gripping the side of the tub and the other placed flat against the tiled wall, Lance continued to drill me like a madman. If only he knew all his efforts were fruitless in pleasuring me. I prayed silently for it to be over soon. After about two more minutes, I redirected my thoughts to something else; I damn sure didn't want to be focused on the bullshit ass scene that was playing out.

To my dismay, the shower had been running so long that there was no more hot water. Needless to say, Lance and I ended another lousy fuck with a stand-up wash at the sink.

The next morning, Lance walked downstairs fully dressed in what he called his Sunday clothes, a sky blue Sean John jogging suit and a pair of hi-top Air Force Ones with the Velcro open…the type of dress that got me hooked on his ass in the first place. I was already up and downstairs with the girls who had woke up an hour earlier than he did. I fixed them some cereal and then set them in front of the television so they could finish watching the movie they had fallen asleep on.

Lance strutted into the kitchen with a smile on his face like he was the fucking man. I wanted to tell him not to brag on himself because he didn't do shit last night but give me a fucking backache, but I held my tongue, not wanting to steal his joy.

I already knew his plan, which was to find a way out of the house and leave me stuck in the house with the kids all day. And just as I thought…he announced he had to go down to the club and make sure everything was okay since he had left early yesterday evening. *Damn, Ms. Cleo's got nothing on me.* He made up some bullshit ass excuse about there being a couple of parties still going on and Bone Thugs N' Harmony making an appearance after he had left, but I could see right through his lies. His real reason for having to leave was his desire not to be at home with the kids. Well, who the hell did I look like…Fran Drescher of *The Nanny*? Lance was certainly taking full advantage of my kindness.

After planting a dry kiss on my cheek, he was out the door with the dust kicking up from beneath his heels.

Selena was supposed to be going home, but I know my husband, and when Lance gets down to that club, he's always gone for hours at a time. And my taking her home was out of the question. I guess you can say I'm not exactly anxious to meet the woman who my husband was committing adultery with. I mean, can you blame me?

Suddenly remembering I was scheduled for a much-needed hair appointment with Heather, my stylist, I called Lance at the club to ask what I was suppose to do with Selena since I was dropping Alexis off at my mother's. Of no surprise to me, he told me to take her with me and that he would be home shortly to pick her up and drop her off at home, which I knew was a lie when the words left his mouth. Selena would either end up staying another night or going home very late.

As I said, I know my husband. At six o'clock, Lance called and asked me to drop Selena off at home by seven because he was overwhelmed with paperwork and couldn't get away. After explaining to him that Alexis had just fallen asleep and that I wasn't going to wake her up just to drop Selena off, he instructed me to wait by the phone for him to call back, and then hung up the phone. Five minutes later, Lance called and informed me that Rosalita would pick Selena up from the house around 6:30 p.m.

Can you say pissed? Why in the hell did he give his ex-lover my home address? Why couldn't Rosalita wait until Alexis woke up and then I could have met her someplace? I know I said I wasn't thrilled about the idea of having to meet her, but I sure as hell would've rather met her somewhere instead of having her come to my home. But it was too late since Lance had already given her the address.

I quickly hung up the phone and headed upstairs, attempting to make myself presentable for the first meeting with my nemesis. After applying some makeup, I removed my heather grey sweat suit and threw on my favorite pair of Express jeans, new snake print, multi-color Nine West sandals, and a strapless tube top from Victoria's Secret. Once dressed, I descended the stairs and peeked in the living room to check on Selena, who was sitting on the floor watching TV. She looked just like a flawless porcelain doll, except for her unkempt braids that were overdue for a redo.

At approximately a quarter to seven, I watched through the blinds as a blue Kia Sephia pulled into the driveway, the house music blasting loudly from its speakers. I knew it was Rosalita, but I waited to go to the door. As she ascended the steps to the porch, I opened the door. Selena ran over, happy to see her mother.

I made sure I was looking fly as hell, but was careful not to overdo myself because then Rosalita probably would have caught on to the fact that I got all made up to impress her.

When I looked at Rosalita, I noticed a cute woman, but not the knock-out, drop-dead gorgeous type I expected. She was wearing tight jeans, a Tommy Hilfiger T-shirt, and a pair of Ked tennis shoes that were also mules. I could see why Selena's hair was the way it was, because Rosalita looked like she hadn't comb her own hair in a couple of days.

Still not comfortable with the situation, I didn't invite Rosalita inside. Instead, I let her stand right on the porch and I stood in the doorway while Selena grabbed her bags and headed toward the door. Before leaving, she told me how much fun she had and that she was glad to have met me. She then asked when she would be coming back over. I told her she would have to call her daddy and discuss that with him.

As they were departing and I was shutting the front door, I overheard Rosalita ask Selena who had touched her hair. I had taken the liberty of redoing Selena's hair in two ponytails while waiting for her mother to arrive. If given more time, I would have given her hair a washing, which it badly needed. While climbing the stairs to go wake Alexis from her nap, I chuckled to myself as they got into the car and drove off.

Chapter 3

Christian

Before Kory and I could have our divorce granted, I was informed by my attorney that we would have to go to counseling prior to any magistrate hearing the case. Now, why is it that on TV people get divorces in fifteen minutes, but I can't get one without some shrink dippin' all in my business? Fuck it, maybe it's a good idea that I do talk to someone. I have been holding a lot of shit inside for a long time, which can't possibly be healthy.

Our first scheduled session was a "get-to-know-you" meeting. Where did we meet? When? How long had we been married? So on and so forth. Basically, we sat there and validated the same stuff we had spent thirty minutes filling out on the questionnaire. Why do they make you waste your time filling those lengthy ass forms out if they aren't going to read it? This counseling thing wasn't getting off to a good start at all.

As if I wasn't frustrated enough about having to be there disclosing all my personal information to a complete stranger, Mr. Kory Jamar Banks, Sr. sat there and painted a perfect ass picture of himself, like he was Bill Cosby, the devoted father and husband. He bragged on how he was a successful business owner. It took everything in my power not to spit in his damn face. I wanted to scream at the top of my lungs, *"We're here to get this divorce right quick; so stop talkin' that irrelevant bullshit, nigga."*

Obviously sensing my irritation at Kory and the tension in the air, Dr. Wardelle quickly wrapped the session up, explaining that we needed to come back separately next time.

"No, we don't, Doc. Anything I got to say, I can say in front of him," I voiced, still trying to get all my insurance company's money's worth out of the visit, since I knew they would be billed for the full hour regardless if he counseled us for the entire hour or not. Still, he thought we would make better progress if we came back at different times.

"Fine, his ass can go. Clear your books, because my appointment starts now," I told Dr. Wardelle as I sat back in the chair, folded my arms across my chest, and refused to leave.

Chapter 4

Karen

I sat out on the patio with a drink in my hand, staring off into the backyard and silently wishing the man talking would hurry and present his quote of what it would cost to cut the trees down and then just leave me be. Last week's rain storm was a beast. It ripped through the city tearing down trees, poles, wires, and even flooding some areas. As a result of its fury, a huge tree and two small ones fell down on our property. Thank God for homeowner's insurance.

"Well, Mrs. Whitman, if you go with our company, we'll have everything hauled away as soon as possible. We'll start the day after tomorrow and have your yard back to the way it was, minus those destroyed trees, within two days," the contractor said.

Oblivious to what he was saying, I signed the papers, not knowing if we were being charged five hundred dollars or five thousand dollars. Hell, what did I care? The insurance was covering it anyway.

My mind had been going in all sorts of directions lately, not being able to concentrate on any one thing. I was so confused, not knowing if I should stay or leave. Either way could be the death of me.

Following the worker's departure, I sat out back for a little while longer before going inside to call Davy at work, informing him of the outcome of the meeting with the tree removal company. We ended up talking on the phone for at least fifteen minutes, something I couldn't remember happening in a very long time.

We're actually laughing, I thought to myself. *Should I go ahead and suggest going out for dinner tonight? Naw, I better not push it. I'll let him take the initiative, if that's what he wants to do.*

"Hey, babe, I was thinking maybe you could call up Romiers and make reservations for tonight around seven o'clock. I think I might try to get out of here a little early."

OH MY GOD! I couldn't believe what I was hearing. It was as if I were sending mental messages. I had heard so much about Romiers. That meant getting dressed up and going to get my hair done. I instantly became excited.

"What time do you think you will be getting home? I want to be home from Vyss before you get here," I said, still excited at the mere fact my husband was taking me out to dinner.

"Vyss? What are you going there for?" Davy asked in a sarcastic tone.

"To get my hair done. I can't step up in Romiers with all this new growth, and the dress I want to wear…"

Before I could utter another word, Davy cut me off by laughing. He laughed so hard, I thought he was choking.

"I said for you to *make* reservations. I didn't say anything about you going."

At that moment, my face crumbled to the floor, my stomach caved in, and my heart stopped beating. I felt like an absolute fool as I slammed the phone down.

How could I be so stupid? I couldn't believe it. Then again, yes, I could. Nothing had changed. I was the same stupid ass who would make excuse after excuse to family and friends when I couldn't come around because of some new bruise or scar he inflicted on me. I was the same stupid ass that covered for him when he knocked my tooth out, telling everyone that during the construction of our home I fell over some lumber. I was the same stupid ass who accepted the women that he paraded in and out of our marriage. Last but not least, I was the same stupid ass that was going to pick up the phone and make reservations for Romiers...a place I'd only hear about. What was I to expect from someone who treated me so cruel? Just last week, during the storm, he beat me to no end. With every crash of thunder came a blow to my body. He took great care not to strike me in the face after the tooth incident, not wanting to blow his undercover woman-beating tendencies. If my twin brother, Kory, were to find out, I'm sure all hell would break loose.

Last week's beating had to be the worse so far. That night, I cried myself to sleep where I lay. I dared not get up for fear that Davy would go off and start beating me again about something else. I awoke the next morning with him kicking me in the ass and ordering me to get my sorry, lazy ass up so I could fix his breakfast before he left for work.

He used to brush off the beatings with the excuse of having had a bad day at work. *Hell, I didn't muthafuckin' work with him, so why did my day have to be bad, also?* I thought to myself.

Chapter 5

Christian

"Christian…is it okay if I call you Christian?"

"Sure."

"Okay, Christian, do you love your husband?"

"Yes, I love Kory, but I am not in love with him anymore. No, I take that back. I'm not sure if I really know how to love. No one ever taught me."

"Christian, love isn't something taught; it's something felt. It's so deep that it aches sometimes. Do you ever feel like that?"

His words hit me where indeed it hurt. "Uh huh, I feel like that about my son. I'm dying inside. I'm not sure if I love Kamryn like that, and I'm not sure if I love Kory…but KJ, my Kory Jr., that's another story."

"Christian, I wouldn't go as far as to say that you don't love your husband and daughter. Right now, you are emotionally handicapped, feeling as though you can't love more than one person. The thing is, you can love both your husband and daughter, and not love your son any less. Do you understand there are different degrees of love?"

Didn't he hear me say I wasn't taught how to love, so how am I supposed to know about the different degrees of love? If they didn't teach it at Dulles School for Girls, or in one of my engineering classes, or online when I was pledging, then there's a good chance I don't know. And what does that have to do with the fact that I am sitting here crying my eyes out while admitting to some stranger that the only person in this world I have ever loved besides Melvin Johnson is Kory Jamar Banks, Jr.? Maybe at one point in time I actually loved my mother, but I'm not too sure.

"No, Dr. Wardelle, I didn't know there were varying degrees of love," is what I wanted to say, but all I could muster up the strength to do was shake my head from side to side.

"Well, Christian, I want you to know that according to your husband's responses on this questionnaire, he loves you very much. He thinks the world of you and acknowledged your strength as a mother, wife, and business partner."

Now ain't that some shit? He wants to acknowledge me on paper, but when it comes time to open his mouth, it's all about him.

An emotionless "oh" was all I could say. I wanted to say good things about Kory, wanted to believe I was there to work on my marriage, but I wasn't. I was there for answers about myself. I wanted to know why ever since birth my life has been fucked up. *Do you have the answer to that question, Dr. Wardelle? Because all this other bullshit ain't helping me one bit.*

"Christian, tell me about your mother," Dr. Wardelle continued.

Since there wasn't much to tell, it didn't take long. Next, we talked about Daddy. I could've gone on all day about him, but that wasn't why I was dishing out a co-pay of fifty dollars per hour to talk to this quack.

Then he asked me about Kory. Well now, that was gonna cost me. Dr. Wardelle was about to get rich off my ass.

"Doc, considering we don't have much time left in this session, I'm going to give you the condensed story of Kory and I. So, here it goes." I inhaled a deep breath and continued. "I saw him. I thought he was cute. He thought the same. We flirted. We had sex. I fell in love. He ended up marrying Mikala. I whiled out, dropped out of school, and started creeping around with him. I wound up falling deeper in love, and as a result, started a business with him so I could be close to him. I ended up getting pregnant, he proposed, and I said yes, although he was still married. Soon, someone else caught my eye. Kory got jealous, whiled out, and I ended up in the hospital after he beat me up in the shop. Kory went to jail. Mikala left him. We got married and had another baby. A lot of shit happened between then and now. I want a divorce. He doesn't. The lawyer told us we had to come to counseling. You said we didn't do well together in counseling, so you told us to come separately. And here I am."

Mind you, I voiced all of this in about twenty seconds flat and was out of breath by the time I finished speaking.

"Wow, you did have a lot to say. Christian, I feel like we're finally making some progress, and I want to suggest that you return for another visit...that is, if you would be willing. I would like to talk to you some more."

Nodding my head, I agreed to return. Hell, what did I have to lose...besides another fifty dollars, of course.

Chapter 6

Karen

Am I to blame?

I keep blaming myself for what happened. If I wasn't out feeling sorry for myself, maybe I would've been home. I could never bring myself to tell Kory, Chris, or Mama that the real reason I was away from home was because I was out getting ice cream to feed my depression over my marriage.

Hell, no one cares about what I'm going through. They only want answers to what happened.

I remember when Kory called. When my cell phone rang, I looked at the number and sent the call straight to voicemail. I didn't feel like talking to anyone. I just wanted to be alone. It wasn't until Mama called that I learned what had happened. "No! No!" I could still hear myself screaming. I couldn't believe this was happening. I lost my breath as I absorbed the information I was hearing, the shocking news sucking the life from my body. Not wanting to believe what I had just been told, I listened to the message Kory left, hoping to hear something different than what I had just heard from my mother. I couldn't bring myself to listen to the entire message. From that moment on, I felt like shit. I could have been there. I could have prevented it from happening. But once again, me being the failure that I am, I was not there when I was needed most…or so they thought.

I called Davy to tell him the news, only to have him tell me he couldn't talk because he was at work. After he disconnected our call, I held the phone up to my ear for what seemed like more than several minutes.

Finally, snapping out of my daze, I hung up the phone, threw on my shoes, and drove to the hospital. While driving, I turned on the Jazz station as tears streamed down my face. I thought about how I was going to survive. This tragedy was something I would have a very hard time coming to terms with, and I doubt I ever will.

I pray one day to have an answer to my question: Am I to blame?

Chapter 7

Christian

I'm just about sick of Kory. I want to care how he feels because I know it's the right thing to do, but I don't. Throughout this entire ordeal everyone's been showing *him* sympathy.

"Poor Kory, over there trying to keep the family together and taking care of poor Chris."

Taking care of me? Where'd they get that bullshit? Kory must have them brainwashed into believing that shit. He only talks a good game, with less than half of it being the truth.

Don't get me wrong, I know he's hurt. But he's laying it on thick. He's not taking care of shit around here the way they think. If it wasn't for Marcella, I don't know what I would do. The shit really hit the fan when I asked Kory for a divorce a few weeks ago. I just want to escape; I must have inherited my mother's trait to run away from situations which I felt were unbearable. No one can understand why I would leave Kamryn behind, but I'm not doing her any good. It hurts me to admit she'd be better off with her dad instead of me. Still, it's true.

Kory has family, and no matter how fucked up they are, they love each other and would do *anything* for one another, including helping him to raise Kam. Me, on the other hand, I don't have anybody. My father did a doozy of a job raising me, so he sure as hell couldn't help Kam.

As for Aunt Whitney, she is too out for self. She'd sell my baby to the next nigga that would come knocking at her door offering the right price. Besides, she isn't speaking to me anyway. I don't have any grandparents that I have a relationship with, so that's not an option. And who in the hell knows where Carmen is, or if she's dead or alive? Even if someone did know where to find her, she hasn't helped me in all these years, so why would I think she'd help me now?

I thought by sending my son to the best school and sports camps, and dressing my kids in designer clothing like Polo, Tommy Hilfiger, Phat Farm, and Sean Jean, that I was a good mother. I kept them clean, hair done and cut, and fed them nothing but good food. KJ would order a rack of fuckin' lamb when we'd go out to dinner, for goodness sake. My kids thought Red Lobster was like going to McDonald's. Eating out to them was going to restaurants like Morton's, The Moxie, and Lawry's.

I scrimped, borrowed, and begged to come up with the money to buy this house, just so my kids could be proud to have their friends over. Let's not speak on birthday parties! For Kamryn's 1st birthday, of which she slept in her stroller most of the time, my customers' kids had a field day stuffing bears and picking out outfits to dress them in, each creation running me damn near sixty-five dollars. For KJ's last party, one of my customers extended her timeshare to us, so I packed up six of KJ's closest friends and we were off on a plane to Disney World.

So as you can see, I thought I was being a good mother by providing my kids with what they wanted. I showed them love the best way I knew how…by lavishing them with material things. Looking back, I now realize all those things didn't constitute me being a good mother.

So, here's another question for you, God: Why did you allow me to conceive? If it's already pre-determined and you *knew* I wasn't going to be a good mother, why did you bless me with two children just to turn around and snatch one away?

Chapter 8

Lance

Rosalita is really working my nerves with the shit she tries to pull. Every time she calls, it has to do with something new that Selena needs. And like a fool, I go running to slap the money in her greedy palms. If it's not new shoes, it's new clothes. If it's not money to pay for some expensive ass summer camp, then it's money for some dance class, horseback riding lesson, or swimming lesson she's enrolled Selena in. It's plain to see that she is taking advantage of me financially.

Prime example, Rosalita showed up one Sunday with a bill for three hundred dollars from the day camp, saying I had to pay the bill because she didn't have the money. Hell, Alexis doesn't even go to places that run three hundred dollars a week. I thought to myself, *"You put her ass in that high-profile camp, not me. So why on God's earth should I be stuck paying the bill?"*

Of course, I paid the bill, but not without bitching first. Well, that was two weeks ago, and I've been getting the bill ever since. Marcella has been trying to get me to go down to Family Division and pay child support through the courts. She says it will be cheaper for us in the long run and everything will be kept on record of what I'm giving Rosalita each month to care for my daughter. I'm highly considering doing just that because I can't even imagine what Rosalita will demand next.

While riding down the interstate on my way to my boy Darnell's house, I popped in Cash Money's CD and fast forwarded to the track, "#1 Stunner". I'm still begging for Darnell's forgiveness after the shit Marcella pulled. He was pissed as fuck at me when Mar crashed her car into his house because she caught me fucking some man at his down low party. Darnell complained I was gonna ruin his reputation by bringing all that drama around his house. I responded by asking him how the hell his reputation was going to be ruined when *I* was the one caught by *my* wife with my pants down, fucking another man.

Darnell is a true friend and the only person I feel comfortable talking to about anything. Even though Darnell is as gay as they come, he keeps a bad bitch on his arm at all times…for appearance sake. In no way is he sexual with any of them, though. Darnell is strictly dickly. We never had any sexual experiences together…and never will for fear that it will destroy the friendship we have built. In fact, he was the one who encouraged me to fuck with Rosalita, because even though I was married, people were starting to talk about my lifestyle and rumors were spreading. I couldn't fuck up my reputation because then, I would be fuckin' up my money. I know he was only trying to look out for me, but boy, look at all the shit I'm up to my neck in now.

At first, I wasn't going to talk to Rosalita, but she kept coming to the club everyday pushing up on me. After a while, it became hard to ignore her advances. My marriage was no secret to her, and she could care less. She basically laid it all out on the table and told me she didn't want me as her man, just as a friend with no strings attached. If droppin' a few dollars and fuckin' Rosalita every now and then was what I had to do to stop the rumors and save my reputation, then it was worth every dime, nickel, penny, and secret rendezvous.

At the beginning, everything was cool. Rosalita was on call anytime I wanted to see her. She would come to the club or sometimes meet me after the club closed. It was pure lust; all we did was fuck. But after a few months, Rosalita started getting real possessive and more demanding of my time. It even got to the point where she wanted me to start taking her out in public, which was totally out of the question. I was still a married man who loved his wife. There was no way I was going to flaunt her ass out in public.

One time, Rosalita and her silly friends came up in the club talking shit. She was making a scene because I hadn't called her in almost two weeks. Of all the nights for her to show up, she had to pick a night when Kory was there. When she saw I was ignoring her, Rosalita picked up a glass from the bar and threw the drink on me. I tried to play it off like she was a regular patron of the club who was drunk and upset because I wouldn't serve her anymore drinks.

Kory looked at me as if to say, *"What the hell is going on?"*

At the time, Marcella and I were having problems, and I damn sure didn't want anyone to think Rosalita was the cause of our problems. It wasn't until after I had banned her from the club and ended many calls to the club with hang-ups that I learned she was pregnant. At first, she wasn't going to keep the baby because I expressed to her that I loved Marcella very much and was not going to leave her. I had to remind her of the "no strings attached" agreement we had made. That was the last conversation I had with her, until she called me one day and said she had just given birth to a baby girl. The shit fucked me up and couldn't have come at a worse time because the problems at home were escalating. There was no way I could tell Marcella about the baby at that time, especially if I still wanted my marriage.

A few months after she had the baby, Rosalita started showing up at the club damn near everyday, threatening to call my wife if I didn't give her money. I never demanded a paternity test because I always believed the baby was mine. Therefore, I did what a real man was supposed to do, and took care of my responsibility.

Everything went smoothly for a couple of years, but then Marcella got pregnant. I was stuck and didn't know how I was going to handle the whole situation. I knew it would break Marcella's heart, and I didn't know how I would be able to face her family. I wanted badly to make my marriage work. Marcella and I were in counseling to fix our marriage, and I felt if there was any chance of that happening, it would be best for me to come clean about everything, including my daughter, Selena.

I pulled into Darnell's driveway right behind the Honda Accord he has been driving for damn near ten years. This man was a damn millionaire and had an old ass Accord sitting in his driveway, which he planned on pushing until the bitch fell apart. I guess that's how the rich stay rich…by not spending their money foolishly.

After exiting my Cadillac Eldorado, I entered the house through the door which was wide open and walked throughout the rooms until I found Darnell in the game room watching a movie. It's not unusual for Darnell to keep his door open when he's not conducting business. When you live in a nice neighborhood, such as he does, you can do that without fear of being robbed or killed for what you have and others are not willing to work hard to obtain.

Upon entering the game room, I crossed in front of the 62-inch television and flopped down on the futon sofa that was adjacent to the black leather loveseat on which Darnell was sitting.

"D, this shit with Rosalita is getting out of control. The bitch has really lost her mind," I said, sighing heavily.

"What happened now, Lance?" Darnell asked while his eyes remained affixed to the screen.

"At first, Rosalita was cool. Yeah, she threatened to tell Marcella, but I knew she wouldn't because she didn't want to lose out on the money she was getting every week."

"Fuck Rosalita's money-hungry ass!"

"D, man, she has really gone over the edge. At first, she would bring Selena over every other weekend, and then she started dropping her off during the week, which meant Marcella or I would have to take Selena to school all the way across town." I leaned forward, resting my arms on my lap and my chin in the palm of my hands.

Darnell looked over at me slowly, shaking his head in disgust. "Lance, you let the shit get out of hand. I told you to use her to save face, not go and have a fucking baby with her. You need to put that bitch in her place, or it will only get worse."

"Let me tell you about what happened recently. Marcella came home and found Selena sitting on the porch all by herself."

"What!" Darnell straightened up on the loveseat from his relaxed position. "You mean to tell me, Rosalita dropped her off without staying to see if she could get in the house?"

"Yup. Selena told Marcella that her mother dropped her off after school." I diverted my eyes toward the television, not really interested in what was on, but more in an attempt to hide my shame of having gotten myself in this fucked up situation.

"That's real messed up, man."

"Marcella didn't get home until after six, so my baby girl was sitting outside on the porch for at least two or three hours," I said, returning to an upright position.

"It's obvious Rosalita don't give a damn," Darnell stated, returning to his relaxed position.

"Rosalita has even started to fuck with Marcella. Marcella has come home several times to find messages from Rosalita saying that she was calling to speak to her husband."

"Who in the fuck is her husband?"

"Man, D, she's talking about me. Rosalita has called and told Marcella to pack her shit and move so she and I can be together. She has left notes on the house, drove past the house late at night calling my name, and all types of wild shit." I rose from the futon and started pacing back and forth in front of it.

"You got a real live one on your hands," Darnell commented, directing his attention back to the movie.

I stopped pacing and exhaled deeply. "But listen to this. The shit went over the edge last week. Marcella, Alexis, and I went out to dinner, and when we pulled in the driveway, Rosalita and Selena were sitting on the porch. Rosalita ran up to me, trying to hug me and saying how worried she was because she hadn't heard from me all day."

"Get the fuck out of here!" Darnell shouted, looking up at me.

"That's when Marcella lost it. She grabbed Rosalita by the hair and they started fighting in the yard. I was enjoying it because Marcella was getting the best of Rosalita, but I jumped in the middle of them to stop it."

"*You* should have beat Rosalita's ass, with her disrespectful shit."

"The next day, Marcella went down to the police station to file a Protection from Abuse order on Rosalita," I said, taking my seat again on the sofa.

"So what does that mean?"

"That means Rosalita cannot have contact with Marcella face to face, by phone, or in writing. The shit is getting out of control. I've decided to go down to child support and file a case. I want to be a part of my daughter's life, but if Rosalita keeps this bullshit up, I'm gonna have to chalk up my visits with Selena. D, man, my life is fucked up," I sighed, leaning back and placing my hands behind my head.

"I have to agree, Lance. I helped you get into some fatal shit that's fucked up," Darnell said while rising to go to the kitchen for beers, which we both were in need of badly.

Chapter 9

Kory

I don't understand why Christian is on this bullshit. After all we've been through, here I was about to enter a room where I have to explain to some psychoanalyzing counselor why my wife wants to divorce me. This makes me think back to what I went through with Mikala. Damn, am I missing the signs as to why my marriages have been unsuccessful? I fought the urge to turn around, get in my truck, and leave. In order to save my marriage, I knew I had to be there. So, here goes nothing.

"Please, have a seat, Mr. Banks. How are you doing?" Dr. Wardelle greeted as we took a seat in two chairs across from one another.

"I'm hanging in there, Doc. You know things aren't the same around the house," I said, throwing up my hands.
"How is Christian doing?" he asked, staring me directly in the eyes.

"Not good at all. We're kind of avoiding each other. She can't stand to be in the same room with me for more than a minute."

"What are your thoughts on the whole situation? How does it make you feel to know your wife doesn't feel comfortable with your presence?" he asked, pressing on while jotting down notes on the lined tablet which rested on his crossed lap.

"Doc, life is fucked up. I mean, these past few weeks have been pure hell. It's to the point now where the silence in the household doesn't bother me anymore. At first, I would get pissed, but now, I just let Christian have her space. Besides, as long as there's silence, we aren't arguing. When Chris gets mad, she can say some hurtful shit. Excuse my language, Doc." Christian would always get on me about cursing, telling me I needed to work on my social skills.

"That's quite alright," Dr. Wardelle said, raising his hand to stop me from apologizing any further. "Mr. Banks, do you love your wife?" he continued.

Now, in my opinion, that was a stupid question. I mean, if I wasn't, I wouldn't be here wasting my valuable time that I could be spending elsewhere doing something more pleasurable. I started to wonder if I had given the impression I didn't love Christian.

"Oh yeah, it's more than love actually. I breathe that woman. I do love her, Doc," I declared, reassuring him as well as myself. "We've been through so much shi…I mean, stuff over the years," I said, catching myself from cursing again. "Christian and I have a history together. After she gave birth to our son, I knew I was going to make her my wife one day. I didn't care who I hurt or what I had to do to make that happen."

I straightened myself up in the chair. I had begun to sweat under my arms as a result of the nervousness I was experiencing from the questions and those yet to come. I prayed my Arrid Extra Dry deodorant would hold up extra, extra, extra well. "I want to know about your family. Tell me about your parents, siblings. How is your relationship with your family?" He scribbled some more notes before returning his gaze to me.

I thought to myself, *I don't want to talk about my family, just my marriage.* However, I went along with the program. "I have a twin sister named Karen. She's married, no kids. We're two minutes apart, with her being the oldest. I feel kind of bad about Karen because she's like the lost sheep in the family. She really doesn't have a place. We're close, but her relationship with our parents is strained, which isolates her most of the time. I'm not sure about her husband. I use to like him. I kicked it with him a few times and thought he was a cool dude at first. But here lately, Karen doesn't seem to be happy." Dr. Wardelle scribbled some more. "Even before all of this happened, she didn't seem right. She's always jumpy. You say the smallest thing to her and she starts crying." I paused, twiddling my thumbs while he continued to scribble. All his damn scribbling was causing me to become more nervous than I already was. I hate the fact of someone writing something about me, and me not knowing exactly what they are writing.

Hesitantly, but wanting to hurry so the session could be over, I continued. "She's always been sensitive, but you'd think she was pregnant as emotional as she's been lately. Then again,

44

she *just might* be pregnant with all the weight she's gaining. But she's always said she didn't want kids, so I don't know, Doc."

"Hmmm…" Dr. Wardelle looked up from his writing tablet.

"I barely see her unless she's watching the kids or throwing a party at her house. Other than that, Karen's out there in her own world. I love her, though. It's something about twins. We're just like…connected. But I ain't here to try to work out her shit right now. I have to work on me and Chris. She's my sister and I love her, but I ain't married to her. My main concerns are Christian and Kamryn Banks."

"You also have a younger sister, don't you?" he asked, totally ignoring my last statement. I didn't know how the discussion of my sisters was helping to save my marriage, but I entertained him with an answer anyway.

"My lil' sister's name is Marcella. Over the last couple of years, Marcella has been the one I've turned to for advice and support. She's married and has a daughter named Alexis. Her husband, Lance, owns a very popular night spot with his old man. I really like Lance and have much respect for him because he's a young black businessman doing his thing. My father always told us that if we ever wanted to have something in life, we had to own something. That may be the reason why I'm not feeling my sister Karen's husband all like that. He seems content just working for a company, instead of starting his own and letting people work for him. It doesn't seem like he has much ambition, and I ain't feeling that."

"Okay," Dr. Wardelle interrupted, "I don't want to focus too much on your sisters' husbands. I want to concentrate on your immediate family. Tell me a little about your parents."

"Growing up, we were what people would call middle class. My parents owned their own home. Both were hard workers. My sisters and I had a lot. We never got into too much trouble while growing up, so there wasn't much of a need for my parents to discipline us very much." I paused, clearing my throat.

"While growing up, I respected my father. I wanted to be just like him. I mean, he provided for my mother, kept order in the house, and took time out to spend with his kids. My mother, on the other hand, put everything she had into raising her kids. She made sure we had the best of everything, because she didn't want us to have to want for anything…or any of her friends' kids to have more than we did. At times, my mother can be a trip. She's a shit starter, but I don't know what I would do without her."

On that note, we concluded our session.

Chapter 10

Christian

Taking Dr. Wardelle's advice, I scheduled another appointment. My second session just so happened to be right after Kory's first one. I actually saw him leaving the building as I turned into the parking lot. Not wanting him to see me, I waited until he had pulled out of the lot before exiting my car.

"Christian, tell me about Kory Banks, Jr."

"I can't," was all I could say. At least, that's what I thought. However, when I started talking about my baby, I couldn't stop.

"I wanted Kory, Sr. so badly, and I knew his wife couldn't have kids. His sister, who's my friend and old college roommate, told me stuff I shouldn't have known, which I used to my advantage. I longed to have a child. I wanted to give my baby what I felt I missed growing up. I plotted to get Kory to have sex with me without a condom, but I didn't have to twist his arm to do so. As soon as I mentioned not wanting him to use a condom because they were starting to irritate me, he whipped it off and never used one again."

"How long did it take for you to get pregnant?" Dr. Wardelle asked while taking notes.

"I didn't get pregnant right away and was starting to fear I couldn't have kids, either. Then I thought maybe Kory, and not Mikala, was the one who was sterile. But finally, after about ten to eleven months of unprotected sex, my period didn't come. When I found out I was pregnant, I felt like the Queen of Sheba. I mean, I was able to give Mr. Hollywood of the city a baby. I knew then that their marriage was over."

"So did you want a baby, or did you want for their marriage to be over?"

"I don't know. I never looked at it like that. I know I loved my son from the moment I found out I was pregnant, though. See, Kory didn't leave Mikala right away, but that didn't matter as much to me as I would have everyone believe. Everyone was talking, '*Oh, Christian's so stupid. Oh, Christian's just in love…yada, yada, yada.*'

"His mother was even all up in my face, thinking she was somehow better than me because she had her kids after she was married. Then, unexpectedly, her attitude changed completely, and she tried offering me help and support. She turned on her own daughter-in-law because of me. I don't know what her reason was for doing so. Maybe it was because she was thrilled her son was finally able to give her a grandchild. But, yeah, I was feeling all big and shit. I embellished my feelings for Kory because I liked the feeling of being important, but even Kory knew it wasn't that deep."

Dr. Wardelle glanced up from the lined tablet and peered at me from over the top of his wire-rimmed glasses.

Needless to say, I suppose my revelation would call for a third visit…and another fifty dollars.

Chapter 11

Kory

This quack was trying to run up in us. I just knew it. He made me make a second appointment, and I saw Chris pulling into the parking lot when I was leaving from my first session. We were paying out the ass for this shit.

"Kory, tell me about your ex-wife," Doc said, looking me directly in the face.

Oh boy, this is going to be a sticky situation. I can't let the quack get all up in my business, I thought to myself.

"Her name is Mikala. I was very good friends with her brother. He kept telling me that she was interested in me, but too shy to say anything. Now you know it's weird for an older brother to be trying to hook his little sister up. I would never do it. But Rob was different. He thought I was a good nigga…I mean person, and he stepped to me with it. I am not a dude who's all caught up on looks, but Mikala is kinda pretty. She always has been. She ain't fly, but sort of plain. However, she's a nice girl." I sat back in my chair with a slight grin.

"Tell me more," he said quickly, interrupting my flow.

"I started taking her out every now and then. I wasn't trying to make anyone my woman. I was young, and I had my share of women. If I was going to settle down, though, I felt it should be with someone like Mikala."

"So, out of the blue, you asked her to marry you?" Doc inquired, looking confused by what I had just told him.

"Not exactly. After her brother Rob was killed, we were both distraught, and I sort of felt like I had to be there for her. I considered myself to be more like a big brother to her, but she didn't look at it that way. She actually proposed to me."

"So you married her out of sympathy?" he said, shaking his head up and down as if he agreed with what I was saying.

"I guess you could say that. I just thought I owed it to Rob to take care of her in his absence." I rubbed the perspiration from my hands onto my jeans.

"That's understandable, Kory, but marriage is serious. You shouldn't marry people out of guilt," he chastised while continuing to write.

"Trust me, I know that now," I responded while readjusting myself in the seat.

"What happened in your marriage, Kory? Did you love Mikala?"

"That's a tough one, Doc. I would hate to say I didn't love her, because that just ain't right, is it?"

"Kory, I am not here to judge you. I want to help you, but first, you must be honest with yourself."

"Naw, Doc, I didn't love her. Who I loved was Rob, and I know he is tossing and turning in his grave right now listening to me tell you I didn't love his sister. I just wanted to do right by Rob. Does that make any sense?" I threw my hands in the air.

"Yes, but why weren't you able to tell your wife at the time how you felt?" He asked the question like it should've been the easiest thing in the world to do.

"Mikala was head over heels in love with me. She wouldn't have listened if I told her."

"But you didn't give her the opportunity to listen," he stated accusingly.

"Doc, all the signs were there. I didn't ask her to marry me in the first place. I had nothing at all to do with the planning of the wedding. At the wedding, I was crying. She and everybody else thought it was because I was so in love, but I was really crying because I knew I was making a mistake. I knew I was messing up her life by messing with her head." I stood up and walked towards the window.

"You spoke of signs. What other signs did you give her that you were unhappy?"

"I'm not proud to admit this, but I made her get four abortions over the course of our marriage. I was never attentive until I got in trouble with her. I only told her I loved her when she threatened to put me out. I didn't buy presents and never sent flowers. Our sex life was okay, but she wasn't freaky enough for me, and when she tried to be, it didn't feel right. I could tell she was only doing it to please me. It got to be so bad that I wouldn't come home for dinner or anything else for that matter," I said while looking out the window.

"Where would you stay?" he asked.

"I had an apartment close to my shop that I rented."

"Your ex-wife didn't have a problem with you staying at the apartment?"

"That's just it, Doc. I didn't care what her problem was. I was trying to get *her* to leave *me*. I thought if she left me, then Rob wouldn't be upset with me. But she wouldn't leave."

"What finally made you two decide to divorce?" he questioned.

Oh boy, here he goes again, getting a little too personal. I settled on giving him the watered down version.

"I had a child outside of my marriage, and Mikala didn't want to deal with that."

"Is this the son you had with Christian, your wife now?" he asked, interrupting me again for the umpteenth time.

"Yes," I turned to him and said.

"When did you start seeing Christian, before or after you were married to Mikala?"

"Before."

"Did you love Christian before marrying Mikala?"

"I'm not sure if I loved her before I got married, but she was everything Mikala wasn't…everything I *didn't* think I was looking for in a wife."

"Please explain."

"Christian is very educated, but you would never know it by looking at her. She's a fly girl, very stylish, trendy, and with much attitude. She is spoiled as all hell. She can be selfish when she wants to be. She's the freak in the bed and lady in the streets that I would assume every dude's looking for. She's totally out for self and could care less about other people at times. She gossips with her little girlfriends. She's a real trip."

"But you like that, I assume?" he asked while putting his pen down.

"You know how they say a man looks for a wife who resembles his mother?"

"Yes."

"My mother and Christian can't stand each other and would never admit it, but they're just alike. I was drawn to her confidence. She lights up a room when she walks in. She dominates the scene wherever she is. The spotlight has to be on her, if that's the way she wants it at the time."

"What else?"

"She's been down for me."

"What do you mean by down for you?"

"Christian doesn't need me. She can definitely hold her own. I told you she is extremely educated. She could have been whatever she wanted to be. She could've chosen from an array of men who wanted to be married to her. But she wanted me. She was with me on the come up and could've cared less what people had to say." I turned back towards the window.

"Uh huh."

"That's it. That's what drew me to Chris. I love the fact that she doesn't care what other people say, or at least she doesn't show it if she does. People kept telling her to leave me alone and that I was no good. People talked about her bad when she opened the shop with me. Chris has good credit. I needed her. She didn't need me. She could've opened up a shop by herself like most women would've. But not her, she didn't care what people were saying and took a chance with this dude."

Chapter 12

Christian

My third session and Dr. Wardelle was another fifty dollars richer.

"What do you mean?" he asked, looking down at his notes and picking up from where we left off at our last session.

I went on to explain why my feelings for Kory were not as deep as some would have thought. "Kory bought me a Benz while his wife was pushing an out-of-date Ford Escort. I lived in a condo running Kory twelve hundred dollars a month, while Mikala struggled as a daycare worker to help pay their mortgage. I owned a business with this man and collected all the money from the stylists, while Kory took the money from his barbers. Only difference is, I pocketed all of my money and Kory used his to pay the bills in the shop."

"So, for you, this was all about fame and money?" he asked as if that was such a bad thing.

"Until KJ came along, it was. When he was born, I could've cared less if Kory dropped dead while fadin' somebody up. I would've stepped right over him and kept on with my day. However, I didn't want to let go of the *fame* that came with being the bitch everybody made me out to be. Then, I met Doug," I disclosed, smoothing down the back of my hair.

"We'll come back to Doug. I want to know what happened after your son was born," Dr. Wardelle said while removing his eyeglasses.

"When KJ was born, I did what I could to provide a good life for him. I wanted to be with him all the time. I wanted to rock him to sleep. I loved when he reached for my face. I was smitten by my own son."

"Christian, in your mind, what happened?" Dr. Wardelle asked cautiously.

Oh boy, I knew exactly where he was going with his line of questioning. This was the part of the session I wanted to avoid, but knew that sooner or later I would have to face it. My insides wanted to scream out in agony. I haven't had to talk about it since "that" day, and purposely avoided it at all cost. However, my running from it was over as I sat facing Dr. Wardelle. I swallowed hard and took several deep breaths.

"Kory and I chose an accountant who basically was trying to bankrupt us. In order to stay afloat, we both had to put in extra hours at the shop. We both decided the best way to do so was to open the shop on Mondays. Only problem was, we had only requested after-school care for KJ Tuesday through Friday. Since there was a waiting list, we were basically depending on family and friends to help us out." I was speaking so quickly, I choked on my own words from having a dry mouth.

"Slow down, Christian, let me get this straight. You and Mr. Banks were experiencing financial difficulties. Therefore, you both decided to work on Mondays, which were regularly scheduled off days, but didn't have a source of childcare for your son, correct?" he confirmed as he handed me a bottled water.

"Yes," I said, choking on my sobs. It felt like someone had walked into my chest and sucked the air right out of my lungs. Talking about it was extremely difficult for me. And I don't know why exactly, but I suddenly wished Kory was there with me.

"Why does that make you so sad?" he asked while looking me directly in my tear-filled eyes.

"Because I shouldn't have cared that we were about to lose the shop. I should have stayed home and been able to pick my baby up from school like I always did. Damn that shop! If I never see it again, it'll be okay. I actually thought about torching it a couple of times," I uttered in a muffled tone.

"Christian, please don't do anything illegal. It's normal to have irrational thoughts after such a trauma, but that's why I am here…to help."

I was silent for a couple of minutes before I continued. "Kory was supposed to be taking a late lunch on this particular Monday and told me he would pick KJ up. Then, I get a phone call from his sister Marcella who tells me Kory called her and asked her to go get KJ. She was stuck in traffic on the freeway, so she wouldn't be able to make it in time. She told me I needed to go get him."

"Christian, slow down. Let's take a break," the doctor suggested, obviously noticing my anxiety.

It's bad when you can feel your own blood pressure rise. I walked out into the lobby and started frantically searching through my purse for the pills the doctor had prescribed to me for my nerves. *Damn, I left them in the car.* I had agreed to let Kory use my car since his car was being serviced on recalls, so he dropped me off and would pick me up at the end of my one-hour session.

I became desperate for something to calm me. I don't smoke, but as a result of my desperation, I made a mad dash to the gift shop in the building's lobby and purchased a pack of Salem Light 100's, chain-smoking three of those cancer sticks before returning to the office. When I sat back down, we continued with the session and I picked up where I had left off.

"I explained to Marcella that I had a shop full of customers and had no idea when Kory was coming back. By the time I arrived at the school, it would've been well after KJ's 3:15 dismissal time." I paused, reaching for tissues from off the doctor's desk.

"The back-up plan we had arranged previously was that on Mondays, if no one had arrived at the school to pick KJ up by three-thirty, he was to walk to his Aunt Karen's house, which was only two blocks from the school. With KJ being eight years old, and with there not being much distance between Karen's house and the school, we felt he was old enough to do such." The tears started to fall faster from my eyes, but I continued. "There was always a crossing guard at the busy intersection, and he only had to cross one side street. The first three Mondays, we followed him undetected in the car to make sure he was capable of walking to her house on his own. I figured he would do as directed on this particular Monday.

"I called Karen to leave a message on her voicemail, informing her that KJ would be there when she arrived home. He knew where the spare key was and knew to go inside and lock the door behind him. I had planned to have Tanisha take the rest of my clients so I could leave and go pick him up within the hour."

I paused again, banging my hand against my forehead a few times in anger. It was getting to be too much for me. I felt like I was suffocating. I placed my head in my hands and allowed the pain to escape my body through my tears while Dr. Wardelle looked on in silence. After about five minutes, I pulled myself together, wiped my face, took a deep breath, and continued.

"The next thing I knew, Mikala, Kory's ex-wife, was calling to tell me to get to the hospital 'cause there had been an accident. All I could think about was my husband. That would explain why he hadn't called since he'd talked to Marcella. What I couldn't figure out was how in the hell Mikala could've known there'd been an accident involving Kory when I didn't.

"With no time to waste, one of my clients offered to drive me to the hospital since I was too upset to drive myself. Once I arrived, I was certain it was Kory who had been hurt or killed because Leslie, his mother, was beside herself, Phil, his father, was wailing, and Mikala looked as if she'd seen a ghost. Before I had a chance to question anyone as to what had happened, a nurse rushed over to me, yanking me by the arm and trying to usher me into a small room. I pulled away, not liking her aggressiveness.

"'Ma'am, we need you to come this way. We need your permission to take Kory off life support,' the nurse had said in a soft, squeaky voice.

"*'What the fuck did she say?'* was the last thing I remember thinking before passing out. Next thing I knew, my daddy was smacking the shit out of me like some madman.

"Once I came to, the nurse continued speaking in her mousy tone that was irritating the fuck out of me at the time. 'Ma'am,' she said, 'we need you to make a decision. The doctors have tried everything and done all they can do. It's just a matter of time.'

"All I could think about was me being a widow before my thirtieth birthday and having to raise two kids alone. I knew I hadn't been the perfect wife, but I tried. I started to wonder if I had even told Kory I loved him the last time we talked.

"I tried to imagine what he was going to look like laying there on the gurney a few rooms down from me. Then a slew of questions flooded my brain. Why did I have to be the one to go in there? Why couldn't Leslie or Phil go? Where were my babies? Why the fuck was Mikala there?

"After my mind finished racing with all types of questions and thoughts, I managed to muster up enough strength to tell the nurse that I needed to talk it over with his mom and dad before I could make a decision.

"'His father already gave us permission. However, he thinks it would be best if the choice be yours,' the nurse informed me.

"'Well, what did his mother say?' I whispered as I looked up at the nurse.

"She stared at me with a sympathetic look upon her face and said, 'Sweetie, you *are* his mother.'"

Chapter 13

Kory

Man, I swear I'm tired of all this counseling bullshit, but I gotta do whatever it takes to make sure Christian gets through this okay, I coached silently to myself.

I walked into the office and sat in the usual spot.

"So, did you feel like you had to marry Christian because you owed her something?" the doctor asked as he flipped through his notes.

It amazes me how this quack can just pick up where we left off as if there hasn't been a week that has passed since our last session.

"Naw, I wouldn't say all that. I do feel like I owe her, but that isn't why I married her. I married her because it felt right. We already had a son together, and I wasn't about to let another dude raise my son. Plus, after a long talk with my sister, I had finally admitted to myself that Chris was the one for me." I smiled at my own words.

"I wasn't right by getting her pregnant and then leaving her to raise my son alone. Think about it. If I hadn't married Christian, my son would've died a bastard. I should've married her when she first told me she was pregnant. Naw, what I should've done was married her *before* I got her pregnant."

"Does it bother you that you weren't married to Christian when Kory, Jr. was born?" he asked while moving the ink pen to rest against his lower lip as if he were in deep thought.

"It didn't at first, but now thinking back, it does. I could've given him more time with us as a family if I would've done right by his mother." I paused for a moment. "Be straight up with me, Doc." I straightened myself up in my seat. "She can't get a divorce if I contest it, right?"

"Why do you ask?"

"I just lost my son. There's *no way* I can take losing her and Kamryn, too."

"When I spoke with your wife, she seemed to think you two could share custody of Kamryn if a divorce should be granted."

"You're not getting it!" I shouted, irritated by the fact that he was not getting my point. "I *can't* get another divorce. I *can't* leave Christian to raise Kamryn by herself. I *can't* raise Kamryn by myself. That's not the way it's supposed to be. I don't really know why my wife doesn't love me anymore, but I'm hoping this is just part of her grief. I know she lost a lot losing KJ.

"It would seem to the outside world that we share the loss, but I gotta keep it real. I have family and friends. Chris doesn't. I lost a son, but Chris lost her entire world. I can't leave her like that. I just can't do it."

"Mr. Banks, they say history repeats itself. Do you think the same scene has replayed itself, but this time the characters have changed? Rob became Kory Jr. and Mikala turned into Christian?"

"Never thought about it that way, but naw, the scene ain't the same because I didn't *want* to disappoint my dude, and I *won't* disappoint my son," I responded while slowly shaking my head from side to side.

Chapter 14

Karen

The next few weeks went by in a blur for me. I tried my best to stay out of Davy's way, but for some odd reason, he was always hanging around me trying to make conversation. I couldn't figure it out, but I knew sooner or later the shit was bound to hit the fan.

The relationship between me, Davy, and Tanisha, my childhood friend, had dwindled down from a sexual liaison to a platonic friendship, which I actually enjoyed. I hadn't had a true sister friend in a long time. Marcella was off doing her own thing. I hadn't talked much to Brandi, my other childhood friend, since she got married and moved to North Carolina. As for Christian, I was trying to stay as far away as possible from her. I knew she partly blamed me for what happened to Kory, Jr., and I wasn't ready to face her just yet. So when Tanisha called and asked me to go to lunch and shopping, I jumped at the chance, no questions asked.

We started the day off with facials, manicures, and pedicures. After the makeovers, Tanisha helped me spruce up my wardrobe with a few new additions. Tanisha watched as I ran from rack to rack, picking up items I wouldn't normally wear. It was like watching a kid in a candy store. We both laughed and giggled the whole time.

Every now and again, I would make a comment about me not thinking Davy would approve of a particular outfit, or what would he think about my skirt being short, but Tanisha reassured me that my selections were fine.

With fifteen hundred dollars spent on my new look, I felt like a princess. I had never done anything so outrageous before. Afterwards, we walked over to The Briggs, a small family-owned deli, for lunch. While waiting for our appetizers, Tanisha thought she would go ahead and ask some questions she'd wanted to ask me for several years.

"Karen, why have you stayed with Davy for so long?" Not prepared for her question, my eyes almost popped out of my head. "I don't know. I guess because I love him."

"But to let him treat you like shit, don't you get tired of that?" Tanisha took a sip of her diet soda while awaiting my response.

"I know, but he's not as bad as you think," I responded, twisting the paper napkin around my finger. "It wasn't always like this. As a matter of fact, lately, he's been acting like he did when we first started going out and he swept me off my feet. Things didn't start going sour until after we were married and he started working that stressful job. I have faith our marriage will survive this phase."

"Phase? Is that what you call getting your ass kicked on a regular? A phase? What is that, Phase I? And I guess Phase II is the hospital, and then it's on to Phase III, the morgue, huh?" Tanisha said with a slightly raised voice.

"Calm down, Tee. Really, things have changed with him. I don't know why, but they have."

Tanisha dropped the subject and we finished up our meals, laughing and talking the afternoon away. Before long, two hours had passed and we decided to make our way home, promising to get together again soon.

When I flew in the house like a whirlwind, Davy almost didn't recognize me. I bet he was asking himself how he allowed himself to miss out on my scrumptious-looking ass for so long. By the stern look on his face, I thought Davy was going to start with his usual nagging bullshit. But to my surprise, he complimented me on my new look, stating how beautiful and young I looked. With the next breath, he wanted to know what the special occasion was. As I walked past him with a smile on my face, I told him I was celebrating life, and then I grabbed my bags and headed upstairs to enjoy the rest of my lovely day.

Chapter 15

Marcella

Enough is enough. And I'd had just about enough.

Rosalita called me at the last minute and asked if I could take Selena to her enrollment test appointment. Did she think I sat around on my ass all day doing nothing? It was her child's future and she couldn't even make time to attend the enrollment appointment. On top of that, Rosalita was enrolling Selena in St. Catherine's, a private school. The girl was only going to kindergarten, for goodness sake. Did she think her child was too good to attend a public school? Hell, I'm the product of public schooling and I turned out just fine, if I must say so myself.

Not wanting to disappoint Selena, I agreed to do it. Besides, it would give me the opportunity to see her once again. When we arrived at the school, or testing center as they called it, the first thing they instructed me to do was sign her in.

"Your mommy will wait out here in the lobby while you take the test," the lady behind the desk told Selena. "After you're finished, your mommy will join you to go over the test results."

Selena never said a word. She just smiled and walked into the room. She was such a lovable, well-mannered, and polite child.

The school's director called me into the office after Selena was finished with the test, introducing herself as Mrs. Reynolds. Damn, she was a tall lady, about six foot one! As tall as she was, she had the nerve to have on a white blouse with too-short sleeves and a pair of flooded navy slacks. She looked kind of goofy, not a person I think the children would take seriously. Her nails were red and oval-shaped, which I thought was out of style along with the Jheri curl she was donning. This was supposed to be a good school and this was the best the director could come to work looking? This couldn't be true.

Mrs. Reynolds informed me that Selena had scored so high on the test she wanted to place her directly in the 1st grade, having her skip kindergarten altogether. With me not being Selena's biological mother, I explained to Mrs. Reynolds that I would have to go home and discuss it with her parents, then have one of them contact her. If Rosalita would've taken an hour out of her day, the decision could've been made right then and there. At that point, the only thing I *could* do was hope Alexis would be as smart.

She was surprised when I informed her that I wasn't Selena's mother, especially since Selena had told her differently while they were in the testing room. I explained to Mrs. Reynolds that I was her stepmother and that Selena came to visit with us often.

Taking Selena to the testing center was one of many things we've done together. Right before school started, I was the one who took Selena shopping for uniforms, shoes, and school supplies. Selena's visits soon increased from every other weekend to *every* weekend. Rosalita got so bold that she started dropping Selena off at the house with a bag full of clothes. A week ago, I pulled up in the driveway to find Selena sitting on the stairs, waiting with her bag.

As soon as we stepped foot in the door, and after sending Selena to play with Alexis, I called Lance. As much as I disliked Rosalita, I didn't want Selena to hear me badmouthing her mother to him. Lance tried to assure me he would take care of everything.

"Bullshit! I'm stepping in this time," I shouted in disgust, not trusting his sorry ass to handle shit.

It's like he had no control over the woman. He let her say and do whatever she damn well pleased. Lance begged me not to call her, and I gave in. I would allow him one last time to prove he was a man by setting her ass straight, or else I was going to handle her my way. Just in case, I made a mental note to call Chris so we could strategize our game plan should this bitch keep trippin'. I knew my sis-in-law was hurting and going through her own things, but she had never been one to back down from a good fight.

Let's get ready to rumble!!!

Chapter 16

Christian

I can't believe Kory told me to give his mammy a break. Give her a break? This woman was telling anyone who would listen, including news reporters, that I should've picked KJ up from school and not allowed him to walk to Karen's house alone. First of all, *Kory* was *supposed* to pick him up. Secondly, how was I supposed to know the crossing guard had left her post early due to a personal emergency, leaving KJ to cross that busy intersection on his own? Do they think I would have actually let my baby walk home alone if I had known?

Leslie seems to have forgotten that I am *not* the one who made the choice for KJ to start walking to Karen's house in the first place. Kory thought I babied KJ too much and would make him "soft". He told me his sisters and him were walking across freeways to get to and from school when they were only in kindergarten. Leslie must have forgotten that shit. Now all of sudden, I'm such an unfit mother because *her* son failed to pick up *my* son from school.

And I'm about sick of her ass carrying on about the street he had to cross. Like I said, I didn't know there wouldn't be a crossing guard, and I damn sure didn't foresee my son getting hit by a car full of teenagers. The girl driving the vehicle was no older than eighteen, and had run the stop sign because the rowdiness of the occupants distracted her from her driving. I must say, she showed remorse for what she had done. However, I don't know if I could ever find it in my heart to forgive her. No punishment is compensation for the life of my son.

Leslie also kept harping on the fact that I wouldn't leave the shop. Well, let me set the record straight. I did not say I *wouldn't* leave the shop. I simply said by the time I made it to his school, KJ would have already left and walked to his Aunt Karen's house. Hell, I could blame Kory for KJ's accident, and I guess in some ways I do, since he was the one late picking him up. I could even blame Leslie for buying him that electronic handheld game, which distracted him from paying attention to the traffic while crossing at the intersection. But what's the use? None of it is going to bring my baby back.

I think the real reason Leslie is trying to put the blame on me is to cover up her own guilt. I truly believe she feels at fault for what happened. After all, *she's* the one who insisted KJ have that damn Gameboy.

I would have *never* bought KJ a Gameboy. But see, you couldn't say "no" to Kory's mama without Kory acting like it was the end of the world. I had KJ enrolled in "real" activities, such as karate and baseball. I wanted him to be disciplined since it seemed like his dad had none and I had lost mine somewhere in the game. Leslie argued I wasn't letting him be a child, and was determined to get him that game he begged her for.

Has anyone at all said anything to her about that? Of course not! No one would dare say anything to Leslie Banks for the shit she does. Although, she ran around talking about me so bad that Marcella and her got into a heated argument where Leslie ended up slapping her across the face and now they are no longer speaking. She even had the nerve to drive over here with her sister two days after the funeral to try and get some of KJ's things as a reminder of him. *I don't think so, Leslie Banks.*

See, she runs shit over there at her house, but I run this household. I pay the bills around here and I call the shots. No one was taking anything of my son's out of my damn house. Actually, I felt bad after sending her and her nosy-ass sister stepping before they even got two feet into the doorway. But you just can't go around ignoring my damn feelings because you're caught up in your own.

I see Kory didn't take his mother's side on that one. He better not had.

Chapter 17

Marcella

What a shocker!!!

Lance actually listened to me for once. He went down to Family Division and opened a case. What was even more shocking is that he asked me to go with him to meet with the caseworker assigned to his case. If it had not been for the last incident we went through with Rosalita, I believe Lance would have kept paying her cash money and took his chance of catching a child support case.

When we entered the building, I took notice that a majority of the people there were women, with a few men sprinkled throughout those waiting to have their names called by the caseworkers. Lance walked up to the receptionist to sign in as I searched for two unoccupied chairs.

Once seated, Lance kept shuffling through all the documentation he had to bring. Those people want to know all your business. He had to bring tax forms from the last two years, any receipts he had from clothes he purchased for Selena, and they even wanted to know if I was working. Lance was already paying child support for Casey, so they already had all of his information on file, which is why I didn't understand their reason for putting him through all of this.

The wait seemed like an eternity. Our appointment was for 1:30 p.m., but we weren't called until 2:15 p.m. A lady, who looked between twenty-eight and thirty years of age, emerged from out of the back offices and called Lance's name. Her body language and tone of voice conveyed she would've rather been somewhere else and doing something more pleasurable. Glad that we were finally being seen, I jumped up before Lance.

"Hello, Mr. Japs. My name is Asia Brown," she greeted as we approached her. "I've been assigned to your case."

"Nice to meet you," Lance said while extending his hand to shake hers. "This is my wife, Marcella Japs."

"Hello."

"Hi," I responded back in an unenthusiastic voice.

"I see you're already in the system, so the process shouldn't take long."

"Correct, I pay $725 per month for my son Casey."

"Well, please, come into my office and have a seat."

Just like I thought, she didn't even need the paperwork. Asia told Lance they would first have to establish paternity. Then once the test result came back, and if it proved Lance was the father, they would send out a letter informing him the amount he would be ordered to pay each month for child support. Asia also told him that since he was self employed, he would be responsible for sending out the payment and making sure it arrived on time each month. After handing us the information on where to report for the paternity testing, we left hand in hand.

Now, it was just a matter of waiting four to six weeks for the result.

Chapter 18

Christian

Why did this woman continue to test me?

Leslie had this warped idea that she was entitled to certain things she'd bought KJ. Here my baby was dead, and she was asking me about some damn shirt, game, toy, or other material thing she had purchased for my son while he was alive.

As if that wasn't bad enough, she had to go and throw an absolute hissy fit at the funeral home when we were making arrangements because she wanted him to wear the suit she'd bought him this past Easter. Again, *I don't think so, Leslie Banks.* My patience was running thin with Kory's ass, too, because he wasn't saying shit. *"Stand up to your fuckin' mama,"* I wanted to scream.

I was going to have my son laid out in what the fuck I wanted him to wear, and it damn sure wasn't going to be some drab ass, gray pinstriped suit she had bought him. So, I went right to the mall and bought my baby a suit in his favorite color, baby blue. I also purchased him a white shirt with a baby blue tie and hanky. I picked me, Kory, and Kamryn up something blue and white to wear, also. Needless to say, Leslie was pissed as hell. Kory, in turn, got pissed at me since I didn't bother to tell his mother what color we were wearing. Hell, if it was that important, he should've told her.

You should have seen them. She and Phil came struttin' up in there wearing gray suits and looking all ticked off. It was the funniest shit. I guess I showed her ass who ran things.

It seemed as if everyone had little consideration for how I wanted to bury my son. Take for instance, Phil's friend who's a friend of a friend, and whose family owns a funeral home. Supposedly, this "friend" sent a message to Phil that cremation was a better way to go because it was a lot cheaper. After Kory and I expressed to Phil that we wanted to have our baby buried, this "friend" still insisted we call him. Hold the fuck up! What's wrong with people? Couldn't he respect our wishes not to have our baby cremated?

Now, let me talk about when the time came to pick out flowers. Why Leslie felt she had to be included when it came to selecting the floral arrangements is beyond me, but she was. She insisted we go to this black-owned floral shop that she and Phil have supported for many years. Giving in, I told Leslie I would meet her there.

The woman who owned the shop seemed nice enough and about business, but I wasn't impressed with the shop itself. The owner instructed me to pick out which spread I wanted and she'd only charge me a flat fee of three hundred dollars for whatever I selected. I guess it was her way of giving back since Leslie and Phil had been loyal to her for all those years. In no way am I complaining. It was very much appreciated.

What I could've done without, though, was her and Leslie's constant comments on what they liked and didn't like.

As I ventured off by myself, trying to distance myself from the both of them, I found the perfect floral spray from Kory and myself. It was made of white roses and had a nice blue satin ribbon on it. Then I chose a little teddy bear spray from Kamryn, which they would place on a small pillow and set inside the coffin.

As I began to fill out the card with what was to be printed on the ribbon, Leslie jumped in my face telling me the ribbon should be printed with the words "Loving Family." Hell, I didn't see no "Loving Family" coming out of their pockets to pay for shit. Therefore, the "Loving Family" could kiss my black ass.

I politely took my card and moved over to the next table away from her as she continued to fuss and curse about me being selfish. I tried to act as if I didn't hear her, but soon, she started to get to me. Next thing I knew, I had started crying right in the middle of the floral shop. The last thing I wanted was for Leslie to know she had gotten the best of me.

Frustrated, I called Kory on his cell, explaining to him between my sobs what was going on.

"Babe, just fill out the card the way you want it to be filled out, pay the lady, and leave. Don't let her get to you, okay? You went in your own car, so there's no reason for you to wait around for Mama. As soon as I drop the paper off to the printer for the memory booklet, I'll be home. Okay? I love you, Chris. Now, do as I say."

Following Kory's instructions, I paid the lady the three hundred dollars and left, leaving Leslie's behind still performing and telling anyone who would listen that I wasn't doing right by the family.

While sobbing in my car, and with thoughts of suicide pushing their way back into my head, I did the only thing I knew to do right then…pray.

Dear God,

I don't know why all of this is happening to me. You said you wouldn't put more on me than I could bear. But right now, I don't believe you. I know this is more than I can bear. I don't have anybody. I don't even have a mother. My daddy has no idea whatsoever what to do. My aunts are fake. I still can't believe Aunt Whit hasn't called. And I don't really have any cousins who I can turn to. My husband isn't even man enough to stand up to his mother, although I know he wants to. I understand, though, he's caught between a rock and a hard place.

I know you're not supposed to become focused on what's lost, but instead focus on what's left. It's just that I don't feel like I have anything left. If you love me, Lord, take me now. I miss my son. I need to be with my son. I had to live without my mother. Please God, don't make me live without my son. Amen.

Another thing upsetting to me was how Leslie totally disregarded my wishes not to have a large social gathering after the service, but rather a small gathering at the church. I didn't want a whole bunch of people at my house. I didn't want people smiling all in my face, telling me everything was going to be alright. I didn't want to hug. I didn't want to kiss. I didn't want people looking at me all pitiful. I also didn't want to have to clean up after a bunch of grown-ass drunken niggas. I just didn't want to endure all that after my son's funeral.

Leslie seemed to be in agreement with me, going as far as to tell me she didn't want a bunch of people up in her house, either. But come to find out, the day of the service, she had a huge party-like set at her house, complete with a DJ, clown, magician, balloons, a cake with KJ's face on it, and a mime painting the kids' faces. *What the fuck?* She had a carnival on the day I buried my baby!

Kory chose not to go to Leslie's "carnival" and stayed home with me and Kam. He made the right choice, because if he had left me at home, I would've been long gone by the time he returned. Of course, his mama hit the roof about Kory not showing up, saying I was controlling Kory and taking him away from her. *Leslie Banks, this is not about you!*

She shouldn't have done it to begin with. I know I can't tell anybody how to run what goes on over at their house, but I just found the whole thing to be disrespectful.

To make matters worse, Mikala was there.

I know she was married to Kory, but she and Leslie weren't close. Leslie never gave a fuck about her, and Mikala knew it. I knew Leslie never really cared for me, either. I guess she felt I wasn't good enough for her son. But he thought differently. Now that I think about it, Leslie never really had any kind words to say about me. I mean, she was cordial when I would come over to visit Marcella, but that's really about it. She tried to act like she liked me when she found out I was pregnant, but that was only to get to my son. I could see right through her. I know when people don't like me, and I don't go out of my way to change their minds.

I can't help but size Mikala up every time I see her. She's such a wreck, mentally and fashionably, and the fact that we share the same last name just fucks with me. I don't know what Kory ever saw in her ass to begin with.

I remember when I found out I was pregnant how Mikala kept pressing Kory to get a blood test. Hell, I did one better for her ass. I demanded we get the oral swab test, which was more accurate and less of a wait for the results. When that bitch came back saying there was a 99.98% chance that Kory was the father, I laughed in her face. She never accepted the fact that Kory had a son outside of their marriage. I can't blame her because I most certainly wouldn't have stood for the shit, but hey.

To sum up everything in a nutshell, I didn't want shit to do with Mikala or Leslie. At one point in time, I had actually thought about forgiving Leslie for the shit her and her sister were saying about me. But then after hearing from Marcella that she was still talking shit and calling me all kinds of bitches, whores, and sluts, I had a change of heart. Hell, wouldn't you?

And another thing, I'm getting my number changed because I'm tired of her leaving messages on my answering machine all the damn time. I don't want to talk. I just lost my son, and you think I want to chit chat with yo' ass? To top it off, she ain't talking about shit. Then she has the nerve to call late at night. *Hell-o, I'm trying to sleep!* Shit, I don't even want to talk to my own so-called friends, let alone someone I know doesn't give two fucks about me.

Chapter 19

Christian

"When you say 'so-called' friends, what exactly do you mean?" Dr. Wardelle asked after I had expressed my anger, frustration, and disappointment over the way Kory's family had behaved during my time of bereavement. "Christian, please tell me about your support system outside of your father and Marcella."

"Tanya, who went to school with me, is Kamryn's godmother. I didn't ask her to be. She just insisted I make her the godparent. I wasn't into the whole 'godparent' thing, but, if she wanted to be her godmother and Kory said it was okay, then so be it."

"Have you talked to Tanya?" Dr. Wardelle asked with a concerned expression upon his face.

I almost cried when he asked me that question. "Do you think she even came over to the house to see about me?" I glared at Dr. Wardelle as if he were the one guilty of abandoning a friend. "Hell no! She was busy getting some type of business off the ground, which was her excuse for not showing *compassion*. She could've given a fuck less what I was going through, let alone show *compassion*, as she calls it."

"Have you thought about calling her?"

"No, but then she calls one day, out of the blue, like I should just run to get on the phone and kick it with her. Bitch, puhleeze! I know all she called me for was to talk about her new business venture. I have a business, so I'm not impressed. Keep in mind, I had just lost my son and was not the least bit interested in hearing about her business. When she called, Kory made up some bullshit ass excuse as to why I would not get on the phone. I told him to tell her the truth, but for some odd reason, he didn't want to hurt her feelings. Fuck her feelings! There aren't too many people whose feelings I even care about right now."

"That's a bold statement to make, don't you think, Christian?" Dr Wardelle asked while removing his glasses.

"Fuck, Tanya. I wouldn't care if she never contacted me again. If she was to see me on the street, I would want her to act like she don't fuckin' know me and I would definitely do the same."

"Is there any other friends you have?"

Do you really want to get me started, Doc, I thought to myself. *You better get some more paper and another pen because you're damn sure gonna need it for all I have to say.*

"Well, there's Samantha. Sam and I talked about everything. She was the one person I could be candid with. We always had some shit going on in our lives, so it didn't bother either of us when we had to get in each other's butts. I remember her telling me nothing good was going to come my way if I kept messing around with another woman's husband.

She was too through when she found out I was pregnant by Kory. Even still, our friendship remained solid."

Dr Wardelle reached for his bottle of water but never took his eyes off me. "Tell me more about Samantha."

"I knew she would be in my corner. At least that's what I thought. Boy, was I highly mistaken. She called me, talking about…talking about…" I sat with a puzzled look. "To be honest, I don't know what the fuck she was talking about. All I know is it had nothing to do with KJ and nothing to do with what she could do to try and ease the pain from my loss. She was just rambling on about some nigga she fucks with, about her inability to find a job, about how much weight she had gained, and a lot of other bullshit that I cared not to hear about at the time. Since she couldn't get a rise out of me, she soon found no time for me either."

"Have you spoken to her again since then?"

"No, but I heard she was in the grocery store telling the damn cashier, of all people, that I had gone crazy. I heard she was telling her that Kory and I were doing drugs. Then she told her she was going to pray for me. Samantha J'Neen Little praying for some damn body! I know I ain't the most religious person in the world, but she is one prayer partner I can do without. Samantha has always had a problem with talking too much. But she's hit an all-time low with the Kroger cashier." I paused in an attempt to calm myself.

Clearing his throat, Dr. Wardelle jotted some notes and then asked, "What did you do in response?"

"I called her and went the fuck off. She couldn't even deny she'd said the shit. She claimed she didn't mean 'hard drugs', but the meds prescribed by the doctor. Yeah right! I wasn't buying that. How in hell did she know *what* the doctor prescribed for me? I get upset every time I think about the shit she was running around saying about me and Kory. I better not catch her ass out on the street 'cause I just might slap the dog shit out of her." By now, the volume of my voice had increased.

"Christian, do you want to take a break, or are you okay with us continuing?"

"I'm okay, Dr Wardelle." I could tell he was getting a little uneasy with all my threats, but hell, he's the professional and supposed to help me. Therefore, I kept on talking.

"Now Jessica is a different story altogether. We weren't what I would consider friends. But she had her son at about the same time I had Kamryn, so we actually formed a circumstantial bond. Kamryn and her little boy would play together a lot and we would take them on a few outings together. We weren't on the same wavelength, but I considered her to be a very good mother, so I would often ask her for advice. We did get close enough that we'd talk on the phone every now and then, but usually it was about the kids or some Islamic event she was trying to get me to attend.

"With her dad being one of the leaders of the Mosque, I thought Jessica would at least be chanting for a sistah. Even though we didn't share the same faith, I knew she was committed to hers, and faith is faith.

"A couple of times I called her just to talk, but she never returned my calls. A week after KJ died, she emailed me and asked me to come to her home for dinner. I found her invitation to be sort of rude since she couldn't even give me the courtesy of a return call. However, I ended up going anyway. The moment I pulled up, I regretted my decision. I immediately noticed Sam and Kendra's cars, two people I certainly didn't feel like seeing.

"During the party, Jessica admitted she'd received my messages but hadn't had the time to call me back. Now what kind of attitude was that to have coming from a religious freak who's always quoting stuff from the Quran. Well, Jessica White could save it for her prayers, Quran reading, confession, or whatever, because I didn't want to hear it. Right then and there, I decided I wasn't going to fuck with her anymore, either."

"Why do you think all of your friends turned their backs on you, as you said?" Dr. Wardelle asked while jotting on his pad, which was quickly becoming filled with notes.

"I don't know, Doc, but I have one more person to tell you about, and it's Kendra's ass. This bitch lived next door to me while I was growing up and was always over my house eating dinner and shit, like she was part of the family. I thought it was cool, because I didn't have any brothers and sisters. She went with us on family vacations sometimes and we played together a lot. She was a little bit older than me. She even let me use her ID when she went away to college so I could get in the clubs with my hot ass.

"Now, when KJ first passed, Kendra was coming over all the damn time, trying to sit with me and everything. She was coming so much, sometimes I'd hide in the house with all the lights off so she'd think I wasn't home. Somehow, she managed to get by Kory a few times. I must say, though, I really did appreciate her company every now and then, even though I knew she didn't have anything better to do. Still, it was certainly more than any of my other 'friends' were doing.

"But soon, she got too comfortable with our friendship and started buggin' out, too, like the time she asked me to watch her kids one weekend while her and Jacob, her boyfriend, went to the Pocono's to celebrate their anniversary. First of all, Kendra had six damn kids. Secondly, she and Jacob weren't even married, so what damn anniversary were they celebrating? I owned a beauty shop, not a damn daycare. I found a way to politely tell her, 'Hell no.'

"Now, everyone knows I am one hell of a cook, with one of my specialties being my peach cobbler. Well, Kendra was having a party at her house in honor of some shit or another, and don't you know this broad had the audacity to call and ask me to bake a peach cobbler for her party? The nerve! She didn't even invite me to the bitch and here she was asking me to donate a cobbler."

I was talking faster than Dr Wardelle could write, but he assured me that he was listening to what I was saying by either nodding his head or giving eye contact when he wanted me to elaborate more.

"Do you think she was asking you to do these things to keep you busy?"

"At first I thought that, but then she started emailing me, talking about every time she went out she saw someone who reminded her of KJ. Hell, I live in a house that reminds me of KJ, I sleep with a man that reminds me of KJ, and when I look in the mirror, I'm reminded of my baby. Did she really think I wanted to hear what she was saying?

"And as if she hadn't did enough damage with her inconsiderate self, one day this heffa went and asked me if it would be too much trouble for me to go up to her kids' school since I was off work and enroll their bad asses in the after-school program. Her reason for wanting to enroll them was because she didn't feel comfortable with them walking home from school alone ever since KJ had been hit.

"By now, I'd had about enough of Kendra's ass. While still on the phone with that black cow, I was in the closet loading my gat, and soon, I was on my way to that bitch's house. She had pushed me to the limit."

"Where was Kory when all of this was taking place?" Dr Wardelle asked while leaning forward in his seat.

"Kory was in the backyard talking to the neighbor when I walked out. I gave him a sweet, forced grin and simply told him I was going for a ride. I went for a ride all right…straight over to her house.

"Once I got there, I banged on that damn door so hard my knuckles were bleeding. I felt no pain, though, and kept on banging. I knew Kendra was inside because her car was parked outside. She was probably scared to answer the door for fear of what stood on the other side…me. I stood outside screaming in an uncontrollable rage for that bitch to come out. From out the corner of my eye, I saw the neighbors peeking through the curtains of their windows and some had even opened their front doors.

"I can't say how long I was out there, but the next thing I knew, Tanya and Sam pulled up, tires screeching. I knew Kendra had called them to her rescue…with her punk ass.

"'Chris, we love you. We understand what you're going through,' Tanya was shouting to me. My question was since none of them had ever lost a child, how could they possibly understand what I was going through?

"'What do you want from us?' she cried. While all of this was taking place, Sam just stood speechless in the distance, as if she was in shock.

"'I don't want shit from y'all, but to leave me the fuck alone!' I shouted. The next thing I knew, Mel came from out of nowhere and tackled me to the ground. Kendra must've placed a call to his ass, too. He knew I wasn't anybody to fuck with and that I'd shoot them bitches and drive away with no problem. I was kind of disappointed in him because I thought he'd have my back. Shit, he should've brought his gat and started shooting.

"While he wrestled the gun out of my hand, Tanya stood there talking shit. 'Chris, you're crazy. Why are you blaming us for what happened?' she said.

"'Shut the fuck up! If it wasn't for my dad standing in my way, I would show your ass just how crazy I am,' I yelled as my daddy literally dragged me to his car. I still have bruises from him dragging me."

"What happened after your father took you to his car?"

"Well, I drove myself home, got in the shower, took two pills, and rested like nothing at all had happened. Kory wasn't there when I returned, and I must have drifted off to sleep quickly because I didn't even hear him when he came home.

"When I woke up, I saw a card on my nightstand from my husband. The outside read: *'If it would help to know that somebody cares…I'm that somebody.'* On the inside, he had written: *'All the reasons why I love you would be almost impossible to express, but the most important to me is that you have touched my heart in a way no one else ever has. I want you to get better. Please let me help you get through this. I feel like I am losing you. I need you, Christian, and only you. I don't feel complete when I feel as if your heart isn't in it. This is not the time for us to divide. Our relationship has been nothing less than wonderful and the things that God has put us through can do nothing but bring us closer and make us stronger. We have a passionate love for one another. We always have (smile). I think constantly about our future. I want you to know I will never leave you and will always love you.*

'P.S. If you look deep inside yourself, you will find a little sunshine to brighten your day. I pray that during these tough

times you will let me be the sunshine in your life, because you will keep my heart glowing forever. Love Always, Kor.'

"After reading the card again for a second time, I got up and crept in Kamryn's room. Even though she was still sleep, I kissed my baby good morning on her forehead. I then returned to the bedroom, locked the door, removed my pajamas, let my hair down, and climbed on top of what's rightfully mine. I think it was the first time either one of us had smiled in the past three weeks. His giving me that card couldn't have happened at a better time."

Looking up from my reverie, I noticed Dr. Wardelle smiling for the first time since we had started the sessions. I took it as a sign that we were making progress…finally.

Chapter 20

Karen

I don't know why Daddy treats me like this. I'm his first born and he acts like I'm not even a part of the family. Anything that Kory or Marcella ask for, they get...no questions asked. But let me even part my lips to ask for something and Daddy says "no" so fast it hurts.

When I was a little girl, I was Daddy's pride and joy. I can recall how Daddy would take me every other Friday when he got paid to Pick Way to buy me some new shoes, and how he stood in line at Gold Circle all night long to buy Monty, my first Cabbage Patch Kid, because I begged him every day for two weeks straight. After Marcella was born, though, everything changed. It seemed like once Marcella was walking and talking, I was no longer the center of attention.

I remember the time when I was ten years old. Daddy bought Marcella and Kory new bikes but I had to ride Kory's old bike, because Daddy said he didn't have enough money and since Kory was the only boy, he deserved to get a new bike and I didn't. What a mean and hurtful thing to say to a child, especially one who is your own flesh and blood.

When I was in high school, I was always referred to as Kory's twin. I hated that. Shit, I have a name. It got so bad that people just started calling me Twin. I always hated being a twin. I wanted my own identity, not be overshadowed by my twin brother.

When I was younger, I was sort of on the chubby side. Daddy would call me Fat Twin. Let me tell you one thing, it doesn't feel good to grow up with everyone making fun of your weight. Daddy would make me do the worse things, like walk to school while Kory would ride the bus. Daddy said he wasn't raising any fat asses and until I lost weight, I was going to be walking everywhere.

On top of being overweight, I wasn't the smartest child, and Daddy would remind me of this every semester when report cards came out. He would rub in my face how smart Marcella was or how nice and thin she was.

As you can see, I have plenty reasons for feeling the way I do…like the black sheep of the family, the outcast, the child no one wanted.

Chapter 21

Christian

After returning home from my counseling session, I decided to call Marcella since I hadn't talked to her in awhile. Kam had been over her house all week and I'd only talked to her twice. Marcella felt I needed some "me time" and I couldn't have agreed with her more.

"Hey, Mar, what's up?" I said when she answered the phone.

"Nothing much. Just watching the children play. Alexis has Kam running around like a chicken with her head cut off. Kam's trying to get the beach ball from her."

"I hope she drops a few pounds while she's doing all that running." With Kam's thick thighs and round, full cheeks, she reminded me of a Butterball turkey, but I loved every pound of her.

"Yeah, right! Are you kidding me? That girl eats everything that isn't nailed down."

We both laughed, and then there was a long period of silence.

Finally, Marcella whispered in a voice which was barely audible to the human ear. "So, how are you doing, Christian?"

"Okay," I uttered quickly, but in a forced upbeat tone.

"Chris, it's me you're talking to…Mar. How are you *really* doing? And don't lie because I've talked to my bighead brother."

We laughed and once again, a strange silence fell over the phone. Then, all of a sudden, I began to cry. It seemed like an eternity passed before the next words were spoken.

"Mar, I…I…I just want to die!" I blurted out of nowhere.

"Please don't say that," Marcella said through her tears.

"It's true. I hate life. I hate not having my son here. I hate not having a mother to comfort me. I hate the young girl who hit and killed my baby. I hate the people on the street for not stopping and helping him. I hate the police who haven't arrested the girl and put her ass in jail, knowing she is dangerous out there on the streets. I hate the doctors who couldn't save him. I hate your mother for…well, just because. I hate Mikala for being the first one to show up at the hospital. I hate the school for not keeping better records and only having Mikala's number to call. I'm a heartbeat away from hating Kory for not picking up KJ like he said he would."

By this point, we were both crying uncontrollably; loud sobs emitted through the telephone wires.

"Chris, you don't mean that."

"Yes, I do. And oh yes, I *definitely* hate myself. I AM A MOTHER…a fucking mother who is supposed to be there to protect my kids! That's what mothers do. I didn't protect KJ. I wasn't the *stay-at-home* mom he always wanted me to be. He was always asking me why the other moms came up to the school to read with the kids, go on field trips, and volunteer at school functions. I just *had* to go to work so we could have nice things and keep up with the Joneses."

"Stop it. You're an excellent mother. Don't ever doubt that."

"How can I be when I didn't protect my own son and I'm questioning whether or not I love my own daughter?"

"Chris, I'm going to let that last comment slide. You're just hurting right now. That's why I came and got Kamryn. You *do* love her. That's the reason you let her come stay with us for awhile. You know you can't give her the attention she needs right now, so you allowed someone else to step in. Alexis has enjoyed having her over and Selena absolutely loves her. Selena thinks she's their mom." Marcella chuckled.

"I'm hurting? I'm hurting? Who gives a damn about how I feel? My baby was hurting when that young, ditzy broad ran him over. Can you imagine the pain he must have endured, Marcella? Can you? Fuck how I feel! I can't think of anything but my baby." I was sobbing even harder now.

"Christian, calm down. You are too worked up to be by yourself. Where's Kor?"

"I don't know and I don't give a fuck. It was his sorry ass who didn't pick my baby up. I hope he's getting hit by a damn car somewhere," I spat into the receiver.

"Chris, that's mean," Marcella said. "If Kory gets hit by a car, you know it'll be just your luck that his ass won't die. Only good thing that would come out of it is he'll probably end up in a wheelchair and then you'll be able to get good parking spaces. Y'all will have one of those big blue ass signs hanging from your rearview mirror with a white fucking wheelchair on it. Imagine his ass trying to cut hair from his chair on wheels. He can forget the Barber of the Year Awards. Girl, he'll have to enter the Special Olympics if he wants any more trophies!"

Damn, I tried hard not to laugh, but Marcella was out of control. I couldn't help it. I burst into laughter, and could hear her ass breathing a sigh of relief.

"Girl, puhleeze!! I'd roll his broke, handicapped ass right on back to Philip and Leslie Banks."

"Shiiiiiit, Chris, you know Mama talk a good game, but she don't want K-Boy back in her house. Hell, she doesn't want any of us back in her house!"

"Well, I guess he'll be over there with you, Baby Boo," I said between my laughter.

"Oh no! I lived with K-Boy all my life and I only saw my brother naked one time. It was by accident and I almost lost my damn mind. Besides, if his ass can't walk, who's gonna wash his funky butt? Ewww! The only person's shitty and pissy accidents I'm going to change are Alexis Monique's. I ain't fuckin' with no grown ass nigga that can't wipe his ass. Fuck that! You better keep rollin' his ass over to his plump ol' twin sister's house."

"You know damn well Davy ain't having that shit."

We were both out of breath from laughter. Marcella and I ended up staying on the phone for over two hours, talking and laughing. We talked so much the battery to her cordless phone went dead before I could even thank her for caring for Kam while I got my shit together.

Marcella is ignorant and she says some of the dumbest shit. I had to threaten to click on her about three damn times during the conversation, but that's my girl. To think I had stopped speaking to her for a long time after Kory and Mikala got married. Now, I swear on everything I don't know what I'd do without her.

Chapter 22

Kory

I did one helluva job fixing up the new shop, if I must say so myself. I purchased a new place closer to the city, making it more accessible to people. Remember, a business' key to being successful has a lot to do with location, location, location. Plus, developers were paying a pretty penny for our old property to create some new shopping plaza in the area, and they couldn't build unless we sold. I felt it was a great business investment and went for it after discussing the details with the family attorney. Vyss Hair Salon and Spa's grand opening was only three weeks away.

Vyss, pronounced Viss, was a character that KJ absolutely adored. I don't know exactly what KJ found so fascinating with him, but I do know his powers came from the sun. Christian and I thought it would be a fitting name since our powers came from *our son*, KJ.

I made Christian hire new stylists and rid the shop of the old hoodrats who used to wash hair. We don't have shampoo girls anymore. Instead, we have personal assistants who wash hair, answer phones, introduce the new customers to the stylists, and handle other miscellaneous duties around the shop. The new shop was designed to give each individual stylist their own personal styling venue, complete with three shampoo bowls, two styling chairs, and four dryers.

Heather Lemak, the white girl I hired, would be the shop's managing stylist and my boy Maurice would continue to manage the barbers. We also welcomed onboard three masseuses and three nail techs. In addition, we would be offering the services of facials and eyebrow arching. Toward the back of the salon is a small café which would be managed by Sharmaine, who would also manage the nail techs and masseuses.

"I need to call this short but informative meeting to order," I said loud enough for everyone to hear. "I need for everyone to grab a seat while my wife and I go over important information all of you need to know. First, I'd like to thank each one of you for all of your hard work in helping us get the shop up and running. You all know this has been an absolute horrible time for Mrs. Banks and me. But we welcome those of you who are new to the family and would like to thank those of you who have been with us since we first started out. Both Christian and I are very business-like and will accept nothing less from all of our employees. We are a team and must always work together as one.

"Marcella Jap, my sister, will be the web manager. We will use the computer system to take credit card and debit payments, keep track of appointments, create schedules, provide customers a private venue to give feedback on our services via our website, and sell retail products online. She will be here tomorrow to go over all the technology information you will need to perform your job efficiently. Now, I will turn the floor over to my wife, Christian."

Christian stood and proceeded to the middle of the floor, clearing her throat.

"Good afternoon, fellow employees. I want to first start off by saying we have many professional contacts. We will be servicing pro-athletes, local news anchors, actresses, actors, models, entertainers, and the like. We are not, and I stress *are not*, in the business of hounding customers. Therefore, harassment for photos and/or autographs will not be tolerated and will be a cause for immediate termination. If one offers you a photo or autograph as a token of their appreciation, it will be totally acceptable.

"As for working attire, all barbers are to wear black underneath their smocks, no exceptions. All stylists are to wear white, not cream, not ivory, and not eggshell. They, too, are required to wear smocks. The techs and masseuses are to wear a combination of black and white. Sharmaine has taken care of ordering smocks for all of you, managers included.

"The shop will be open for business seven days a week, eleven hours a day. Business hours will be from 7 a.m. to 6 p.m. Please don't schedule your final appointment after 4:30 p.m. unless you discuss it with your manager first, as they can't leave until after you have cleaned your workstation and exited the building. Each employee makes their own work schedule, but must work five out of seven days and at least forty-five hours a week. Saturdays and Sundays are rotating shifts. Christian and I will post the rotation schedule in the break room on the 25th of each month.

"The Employee of the Month will be chosen based upon customer reviews, percentage of dollar sales, and enhancements. Therefore, suggestive selling is encouraged. Overall, attitude and willingness to be flexible in a high-volume shop is rewarded. If selected, you will receive a $250 bonus in your next paycheck, a designated parking spot for the month, and one additional paid vacation day. Quarterly payouts will be based on meeting the service goals created and managed by Kory and me."

Christian paused to take a breath and switch her weight from one leg to the other.

"If you are resigning from your position here at Vyss, please give your resignation letter to your manager four weeks in advance. If you fail to do so, you will still be responsible for two months' booth rent and will *not* be given a recommendation letter. A notarized contract will be given to you tomorrow when the business manager arrives.

"The answers to most questions or concerns you may have that I haven't answered may be found in your employee handbook you were given upon being hired. Any that are not addressed in the handbook may be directed to Kory or me either at the beginning of the workday or at the end of your scheduled shift. Any questions?"

Everyone looked around at one another. Then, I could hear their asses whispering to each other, "She runs a tight ship."

That's my wife, all right, I thought to myself, a broad grin on my face. *And I love her with every breath in my body.*

Chapter 23

Christian

As Kory returned to the shop after having been gone for less than an hour, he walked in and introduced everyone to Mrs. Newman, our new accountant, who had appointments set up with each of our employees to discuss taxes, checking and savings accounts, IRA's, 401K, and other financial issues. While waiting for their turn to meet with her, the employees busied themselves with decorating their styling rooms.

"Hey, babe," I said flirtatiously as Kory kissed me on the cheek.

"I came to introduce Mrs. Newman to everyone and take my lovely wife out to lunch." He looked at me with a devilish grin.

"Which of these women is your wife?" I asked teasingly.

"She's part owner of this here juke joint. About 5'1", 120 pounds, delicious titties, a fat ass, and the best pus…"

"Koooory!" I screamed to drown him out. "Shuuut up!"

"Well, you asked," he said, still looking devilish.

"Well, let me see if I can find the Mrs. for you, handsome. I'll be right back."

I must give it to him. Kory had been trying really hard to work on our marriage. Since we couldn't find the time to attend the counseling session because of our busy schedule with trying to get the new salon open, we didn't meet our required minimum attendance and the divorce had to be put on hold. Kory was trying everything in his power to keep me from pursuing it. We've been so busy dealing with KJ's death, the opening of the new shop, and caring for Kamryn that I actually hadn't had the time to talk to the lawyer about anything concerning the divorce. Although, I still feel I may proceed with it.

After applying a fresh coat of my new Christopher Lip Gloss, touching up my powder, and throwing my sunglasses on top of my head, I sashayed out to meet my husband for lunch. He looked like he could've eaten my ass up right there in the shop in front of everybody. It actually turned me on. Before leaving, I instructed Heather to call me on my cell phone when Mrs. Newman was finished meeting with everyone.

While we were walking toward the truck, Kory grabbed my arm.

"Babe, let's walk. I heard there are a lot of nice bistros down here."

I guess the look in my eyes told him I thought it was a good idea. We walked in silence, hand in hand, admiring the sights. There was no need for words. If we saw something of interest, we just squeezed one another's hand and laughed a little. He even leaned down and picked me a flower from a flower bed on the corner. How romantic! Kory and I hadn't been like this since I was in school. I must admit I liked the feeling I was experiencing.

A vendor on the street asked if we wanted to pose for a picture in front of a fountain. They were only five dollars and would be ready in two minutes. We ended up taking ten pictures, with some of the poses being silly. Kory handed the man a hundred-dollar bill and told him to keep the change. Now, you know he must've been in a good mood. I couldn't lie…so was I.

We found a nice little restaurant on the corner of Canal and Vine, where we sat outside at a small table eating deli sandwiches and sharing a slice of cheesecake for dessert. We sat there for hours talking. Not about anything serious, just enjoying one another's company and conversation.

During our conversation, my cell phone rang.

"Christian Banks," I answered in my professional tone.

"Mrs. Banks, this is Heather. I was calling to inform you and Mr. Banks that I had to turn the media away twice since you've been gone. Also, Mrs. Newman only has to meet with Jasmine, Frank, and Michelle. She said she'll be done within the hour, so do you want me to lock up or wait for you here?"

"Babe, do you want Heather to lock up the shop or are we going back there any time soon? Mrs. Newman is going to be done in an hour and the media's been up there," I told Kory while covering the phone with my palm.

Kory had a disgusted look on his face, which I clearly took as *'we're on our way.'*

I placed the phone back up to my mouth. "We're on our way, Heather. Thanks for calling."

Kory was still looking cross, and I knew it was because of the media hounding us. They have been harassing us for interviews, pictures, anything we would give them. They were everywhere…the hospital, the funeral home, our home, the church, the cemetery, Karen's house, Marcella's house, JAPS nightclub, and yes, even Leslie's house. Their persistence didn't get to me anymore. I refused to give into their pestering.

Kory, on the other hand, got so fucked up when it came to dealing with the media or reading the stories they printed. He somehow felt guilty…I guess as though he was letting me take the heat for some shit he knew was essentially no one's fault other than the bitch who was driving the car. However, if they were going to blame me, he knew they should be blaming him, as well.

I guess he was scared one day I would go to the media and give them an interview about what really happened with picking KJ up from school that dreadful day. But what would be the point? Kory loved KJ. He still does. He did everything for our baby. Kory didn't mean to cause him any harm anymore than I did. We both made a poor decision, but that didn't mean either one of us was a bad parent or bad person for that matter.

"Babe, we're almost back to the shop and you haven't said a word. What's wrong?" I asked as I yanked on his hand for him to slow down walking and face me. He shook his head as if to imply nothing was wrong.

"Kory, stop for a minute. Damn, I'm trying to talk to you." By now, I was agitated.

"It's just that every time the media shows up, a new story comes out. Ever since my mother gave them an interview, they're really hounding our asses. I hadn't been telling you, but they've been to the new and old shop every damn day. Mel and Marcella said they have been posted outside of their houses just waiting for someone to talk to them. I know no one wants to say anything, but it's getting to be a lot to deal with. Hell, it's getting to be too much for me. What really fucks with me is I can't stand the things they say about you. But I don't want to give them the satisfaction of interviewing me."

"I know, babe, but it's alright," I tried to assure him, stroking his shoulder. "It's okay, because nothing they could ever say about me will hurt worse than the pain of losing my son."

"No, it's not okay." Now he was the one agitated. "Chris, I think we're going to have to go on TV as a family, stand united, and tell the story the way it really happened. KJ won't rest until we do, and that's not okay with me. I didn't protect him like I should have, and now I'm not protecting you. I know my mother is going to have a hissy fit, but I can't worry about her right now. I'm trying to deal with the death of my son and keep my marriage together." He sighed heavily.

"Whatever, you think is best, Kor." I kissed him reassuringly on the cheek.

While continuing on our way to the shop, Kory suggested I go visit Mayor Amir prior to us doing the interview. He felt Amir could give up some helpful pointers on how to handle the media and not allow them to misconstrue our words.

Mayor Amir and his wife, Tai, were very down-to-earth people who helped us seal the deal on selling the old shop and buying the new one closer to the city. However, Kory was not aware of the advancements the mayor had made toward me. If he had, I'm sure he wouldn't have made the suggestion for me to go pay the mayor a visit, at least not alone. For instance, last year when Kory and I took a cruise with Amir and Tai, Amir would often be up in my personal space, feeling on me, and whispering in my ear whenever Tai and Kory were not around.

Now, being the damn freak I am, it doesn't take much to turn me on. Besides, Kory and I weren't on the best of terms at the time. Needless to say, Mayor Amir's advancements were tempting to me, but I tried to maintain some decency. I had to keep reminding myself that I was a married woman and to behave as such. Several times during the cruise, I had to remind Amir that he was the mayor and was jeopardizing his position if he and I were to be caught in the act. He would simply laugh me off as if he was not the least bit worried about the repercussions of his actions.

Up to this very day, whenever we would go out with Amir and Tai, he'd try some shit, which was the reason why I didn't feel comfortable with going to visit him by myself.

Within minutes, we were back at the shop. Mrs. Newman was finishing up her meeting with Michelle, and Heather, who was singing Mrs. Newman's praises, pointed to the file cabinet where copies of the paperwork had been placed.

"Well, that's it, boss. I'm leaving now," Heather announced. I nodded her a good-bye and joined Kory as he walked Mrs. Newman, Heather, and Michelle to the front door.

After locking the door and pulling the blinds shut, he spun around and proceeded to turn off the lights and turn on the radio. *Shit, R. Kelly is singing some shit about pulling a switcheroo and strippin' for some damn body.* Kory is looking fine as hell. *Hell, we can pull a strip switch off in this mutha alright.* I started strip dancing seductively for my husband.

Before long, he was on his knees behind me, playing with my thong using his tongue, and the shit felt soooooo good. With my thong off, I turned around and dropped to my knees, unlatching his belt. Now I was stripping his ass. He had on the boxer briefs I loved and he smelled damn good.

After pulling them off with my teeth, I pushed his ass back on the receptionist's desk and started lickin' his nut sack just the way he liked it. It took me about three minutes before I reached his shaft and he was hittin' the back of my throat. Kory's facial expression showed the pleasure he was experiencing…forehead wrinkled, eyes closed tight. My eyes remained open; I liked to see the effect I was having on him. I felt like a dick sucking pro, and I ain't even into the shit all like that.

I used to be scared of the dick, now I put lips to the shit.

As he exploded, I did a Lil' Kim on his ass and swallowed his babies. Seeing me do this turned Kory on even more. He threw my ass down on that damn floor and started fisting me. Then he got down there and licked my ass like a damn strawberry cone. After he had tossed my salad, we assumed the 69 position, slurping and sucking as if there were no tomorrow. Once I climaxed, I spun around and rode his ass like I was at a damn rodeo, bucking and swinging my arms about wildly. Not wanting to cum just yet, he threw my ass into a doggy-style position. This way, he had more control. After exploding deep inside me, he whispered in my ear, "You know that's our next baby."

Exhausted, we went to sleep right there on the floor. When I woke up, I knew then I was going to have to ask Marcella to go with me to Mayor Amir's office. I just couldn't go alone. My husband was trying to have another baby, and I couldn't get caught up trickin' with the mayor, then ending up pregnant and not knowing who the father was.

Hell, we were already receiving extensive media coverage, and I'd die if they got a hold to some shit like that. Kory would never forgive me. Hell, I don't even think I could forgive myself if I allowed it to happen.

If Marcella couldn't go with me, then Kory would have to go. I would come up with some reason for me needing him to go with me. One thing was for sure…I *could not* go alone.

Before even putting my panties back on, I grabbed my cell phone out of my purse and dialed Marcella's number.

"Hey, girl, whatcha doin' before you come up here tomorrow?"

"Nothing. I'm just preparing for the training of your employees. Why? What's up?"

"I need you to come with me to City Hall. I need to discuss something with Mr. Mayor. I will tell you about it later."

"What time?" Marcella asked.

"I don't know, but I'll call you in the morning."

"Okay."

"Thanks, girl. You're a lifesaver, as usual. Give Alexis and Kam a kiss for me, okay?" I said as I wriggled my thongs up over my hips.

"You got it. Two kisses coming right up for the little ones." We both giggled. "Where's Kory?"

"Sleep on the damn floor."

"Sleep on the floor? Never mind, I'm not even going to ask." Marcella chuckled slightly.

"I'm about to wake him up, though, 'cause I've got to go over my daddy's tonight. As a matter of fact, it's been a minute since he's seen Kam, so I'm going to come get her and take her over there with me."

"Okay, I'll get her ready."

"I'll be there in fifteen minutes. Naw, make that twenty," I said while looking down at Kory, wishing I had time for a second round of lovemaking.

Chapter 24

Kory

"Hey, Kor! What you doing over here?" Marcella asked as I walked up Mama's driveway.

"Is Kamryn in there? I miss my baby."

"Naw, Chris came and picked her up before she went to Mel's."

"Well, I'm glad to hear Chris picked Kam up. It tells me one, that Chris is getting better, and two, I'll be able to see my little girl tonight."

As I entered the house, I yelled up the stairs to get Leslie's tail moving. "Maaaaaaaa!"

"Kory, you don't have to be so loud. Damn," Marcella snapped.

"Shut it up," I shot back.

As my mother descended the stairs, she reminded me of a contestant in a Ms. Mature Black America Contest. "What y'all two down here fussing about now?"

"Why does he have to be so loud?" Marcella said, whining as if she were two years old.

"Kory, what you call me like that for?" Mama asked, like I had interrupted her from something important.

"Mama, me and Chris talked, and we both agreed we have no other choice but to give the press an interview."

"Well, where is *Ms. Chrissy?*" she asked sarcastically, not appearing thrilled by my news.

"*Christian* is at Mel's explaining things to him."

"She didn't want to come over here, huh?" Mama said while turning up her nose.

"Does it matter if Christian is here or not?" Marcella jumped in. "I mean, really, give it a break," she said, obviously still upset with Mama because of their last argument.

"I don't know who you think you're talking to, Missy. I thought I told you not to come back up in here anyway. Didn't I tell you that?" Mama said, now looking at my baby sister the same way she'd just looked at me.

"Un-huh," Marcella said under her breath as she rolled her eyes at Mama. "But I'm here to talk to my daddy. Where is he anyway? This is still my daddy's house, ain't it?"

"You think you so damn smart, find him." Mama was irritated now.

I can't lie. Secretly, I loved it when Marcella got in her butt. No one would ever challenge Mama like Marcella. She did it while we were growing up and she hasn't stopped. If Karen or I had talked to Mama like that, she would have slapped the dog shit out of us, but not Marcella.

Plus, by Marcella being the baby, she was definitely a daddy's girl, and my old man let Marcella get away with any and everything. I'm a mama's boy for sure, and that's why I went over and planted a big wet one on her cheek. I knew she wasn't too happy with me right then, and that it would be only a matter of time before she'd be throwing my black ass out, too.

"Where's twin, Kory?" Mama asked, as if I would know. No one ever knew where the hell Karen was at. She'd always been on her own agenda.

"I dunno," I replied while shrugging my shoulders.

"Is she going on television, too?" Mama asked.

"I don't know. I haven't talked to her yet. I think Chris said she was going to call and ask her to meet us over here today."

"How is Chris gonna invite somebody over to *my* house and her high pollutin' tail ain't even over here? Your sister doesn't need to be goin' on TV no way."

"Why not?" I asked.

"She's fat already, and being on television only adds more pounds to you. Lord knows she doesn't need to appear any larger than what she already is," Mama said, serious as a heart attack.

"Mama! Get off Karen's back! Damn!" Marcella shouted while entering back into the living room. "Why you worried about what Karen looks like anyway? Davy ain't complaining."

"First of all, Marcella Monique Jap, why are you all up in me and your brother's conversation? I thought you were going to find your daddy. And you're gonna watch how you talk to me when you're in my house."

"Daddy's sleep," Marcella said sharply.

"Well, wake him up or something. Just get out of our business and out of my face." If looks could kill, Mama would have been in jail for first-degree murder.

"I'm not waking Daddy up," she responded with her hands on her hips. Marcella was really giving Mama hell today. Mama just stood there in her robe with one hand on the couch and the other around her coffee mug, looking like she wanted to throw it at her.

As I stood looking at Mama, I took notice of her beauty. Her skin tone was unblemished and a golden bronze, as if she had been tanning. Her salt and pepper hair, which was cut short, was shiny as polished silver. Her teeth were perfect and sparkling white. Her hands were perfectly manicured and her pedicured toes matched. Mama had even lost weight, which could probably be contributed to all the stress she had been under since KJ's death. I always knew my mom was a nice looking woman, but I must say Ms. Leslie had really done a good job of taking care of herself. She is *beautiful*. I see why my dad puts up with her nagging.

Marcella hated to admit it, but she's the spitting image of Mama. Only difference is she's a little shorter, but only a little. They act just alike, too, which is why they can't get along. Marcella wasn't blessed with Mama's teeth. Unfortunately, she had a metal mouth when she was younger. And acne had her fucked up for a few years. Still, she and Mama resembled each other very much. I think that's why Daddy always favored Marcella over Karen.

Don't get me wrong. Karen's beautiful, too. She's actually the prettier of the two girls. She has the thickest hair I've ever seen, and her skin is also flawless like Mama's. She sort of looks like a Black Jap, but she ain't. She's all Negro! Karen's only flaw is her weight. Then again, Mama's sisters are big, so I guess you can say Karen got it honestly.

Speaking of the devil…Karen entered the house, strolling right over to me.

"Hey, Twin," I said, giving Karen a kiss on the cheek.

She hugged me tight in return. She was in pain. I could feel it through our hug. Twins can sense when something is wrong with the other. Instead of letting her go, I kept hugging her, which I felt she needed and wanted more than anything else. I realized then I hadn't seen much of Karen since the accident. Subconsciously, I had been blaming her for KJ's accident and distancing myself from her, even though I knew it wasn't right.

"Twin, is dat you?" Mama yelled from upstairs, having gone to check on Daddy.

"Yes, Mama, it's me," Karen yelled back. "Kor, I saw Marcella's car outside. Where is she?"

"She's somewhere getting all in everybody's business; that's where she is," Mama started as she descended the stairs and entered the living room. "I told her the other day not to bring her snooty ass back around here. I don't know what's wrong with that girl. She thinks she can talk to me any way she damn well pleases. I'm the mama in this house…"

She went on for another minute or so until Marcella popped in from the kitchen that housed the greasy peach and orange wallpaper.

"Hey, sis," she said, walking over and giving her a hug, obviously glad to see Karen.

After they broke their embrace, Karen walked into the family room and sat down on the velvet sectional. Marcella, Momma, and I followed closely behind her.

By this time, Daddy had made his way down the steps, wearing a baseball cap with pajamas. Straight gangsta and old school fo' sho! He took a seat on the other side of Karen.

"What's up, y'all?" he said, yawning.

Although it was obvious he wasn't talking to her, Mama jumped in before any of us could say a word. "Well, Kory and Christian are going on television to do an interview about what happened to KJ."

Daddy shook his head. "Sounds like a good idea to me. When y'all going?"

"Soon, I hope. We want to get it over with. We plan on having them come out to our house for the interview so they can let us carry on our lives in peace."

"Amen!" Karen and Marcella responded in unison.
Marcella turned and faced Karen. "So are you going to be there to tell your side of the story?"

"I guess. I just hope they don't start asking me a whole bunch of questions. I'm hoping Davy will be there, too. That should help ease my nervousness somewhat. I don't like talking in front of people, but I'll definitely be there for support," Karen replied.

Not having talked to Chris since arriving at Mama's, I pulled out my cell phone to call her.

"Babe?"

"What's up?" she answered.

"Karen said she's definitely coming for the interview, but she's not sure about Davy. Are you still at Mel's?"

"No, I'm on my way to Walgreen's to pick up my prescription. You need anything?"

"No, ma'am."

"I saw Kendra when I was leaving my dad's," Christian said in a voice reeking disgust.

"You two didn't get into it, did you?"

"Just a little bit."

"Uh-huh, I'm hip to your *just a little bit*," I chuckled.

"How long will it be before you leave your parents' house? I hope the reporters aren't out front of our house. I have Kam with me."

I hadn't even thought about that possibility. "I'm on my way. I'll probably beat you there, but if I don't, wait until I get there before turning into the driveway, okay? The garage might not open because it was acting up earlier today. If there are some reporters in our driveway when I get home, I'll just run the muthafuckas over."

"Got it, dude!" she said while laughing at my exaggeration.

"Love you," I said loud enough to get Mama's attention.

"Love ya back."

I pushed the end button on my phone and rose from my seat. Walking over, I shook Dad's hand, kissed Marcella and Twin on the cheek, and then approached Mama, who gave me "the hand" before I could reach her. Keeping my distance, I blew her a kiss and started singing "A Song for Mama" by Boyz II Men. Everybody laughed at my ill attempt at singing. Even Mama broke out into a chuckle.

"Love you, Mama," I said as I walked out the door.

As I pulled away and was driving down the street, I looked down and saw the light on my phone blinking.

"What up?"

"Kor, did you see how Mama and Daddy really weren't studdin' each other?"

It was Marcella on the line. I guess she left right after me, because there was no way she would've been having that conversation with them listening in.

"Yeah, but you know Mama is still through with the old man for that cheating shit he did with Sabrina."

"Yeah, I know. I can't believe Daddy did that."

Now I feel dumb, because I'm just as guilty. Therefore, I don't say anything.

"I'm sorry, Kor. I didn't mean to bring it up. Is Chris still upset with you about it?" she asked out of complete concern.

"Don't apologize. Chris is mad at me for so much shit nowadays that I guess you can add that to the list, too. She ain't brought it up in awhile, though. I don't think she's even had time to process it all. Even though things went down the way they did, she still took it hard when Sabrina died."

"Kory, why do you think Daddy did that?"

"Because it was there for the taking, Marcella. Sabrina put it all up in every niggas' face, and Daddy was just one of the cats who jumped on it."

"But Daddy is married," she whined.

"I know…I know. I never said it was the right thing to do. He made a mistake. The man makes a mistake…the mistake doesn't make the man. Don't think Daddy loves Mama any less because he had sex with somebody else," I counterattacked in my father's defense...and in a way, my own defense, as well.

"You would know. I mean, you cheated on Mikala the whole time you were married to her with Christian. You ain't shit."

"Aahh, lil' sis, what I did was totally different from what Daddy got himself involved in."

"How so?"

"Mikala and I didn't have a family or a future; I didn't have love for her in that way. Chris wasn't just a piece of ass to me. It's different."

"Okay, that explains why you cheated on Mikala, but why did you cheat on Chris if you love her so much?" she asked. "Kory, have you cheated on Christian since you two have been married?"

"Nope."

"You answered too quick, nigga."

"For real, I ain't lying. I've been with so many women that it's not a challenge for me anymore. I know those tricks' game. After that video tape came out and all that shit went down with Sabrina, I poured my pimp juice down the fucking drain!"

We both burst into an uncontrollable laughter.

Hell, I didn't know why Marcella was trying to act all prim and proper. Christian had told me about the time they caught Lance cheating. She never told me the whole story because I was mad as fuck she even got involved, but I knew he crept out a time or two on Marcella. Maybe the real reason she was asking all these questions is not because she wanted to know about me and my old man, but because she wanted to know what drove her man to do what the fuck *he* did.

"Well, Baby Boo, I'm pulling into my driveway. Thank God no reporters are out here. Do me a favor, though. Call Twin and check on her. She doesn't look right."

"*You* check on her. She's *your* damn twin."

"Just check on her, Marcella," I said, lowering my voice to get my point across.

"Bye, boy," she said while huffing, a clear indication that she would do as I said.

"Peace, Baby Boo."

After exiting my vehicle, I unlocked the gate. While walking to the deck, I decided not to go inside the house. Instead, I sat and enjoyed the night air while waiting for my wife and daughter to come home. I missed them both so much and couldn't wait to lay my eyes on them again.

Chapter 25

Christian

When I got home yesterday, Kory was waiting outside on the deck, looking as if he was in a trance. I don't even think he noticed us when we pulled up. Kamryn was sleep, so I didn't honk at him. As I was getting Kamryn out of the backseat, he finally jumped up, ran over to fight with the garage door, and then came over to take Kamryn out of my arm while I pulled the car into the garage. After parking, I popped the trunk and took out the bags from the grocery store.

"Kor, are you hungry?" I shouted into the next room.

"Naw, I'm cool. I grabbed something earlier," he said as he entered the kitchen and eyed all the bags after laying Kamryn in her bed. He'd given up saying anything to me about my excessive spending. Now, he just shakes his head.

"So what did Mel say about the interview?" Kory asked while opening a bag of potato chips instead of putting them in the junk food cabinet.

"He thinks we should do it. He's behind us one hundred percent. Karen said she'll be there, right?" I asked while taking the chips from him and putting them away. If I recalled correctly, he said he wasn't hungry.

With a mouth full of chips, he said, "Yeah, but she doesn't know about Davy, though."

"What's up with those two? I ain't seen Davy since the funeral, and before that, I hadn't seen him in like forever," I asked, leaning up against the kitchen counter.

"I don't know, but Twin was looking bad. I mean, she's putting on more weight, and you know Mama don't make it no better."

"Yeah, I know." I just couldn't figure out why Phil and Leslie hadn't learned to accept Karen for who she was, weight problem and all. "Are Leslie and Phil getting along better over there?" I asked, being nosy.

"That's...ugh...I don't know. Mar said she sensed tension. In my opinion, Mama was just acting like she always does. Daddy ain't say too much, but I did notice he ignored everything she said."

"Good for him," I said while applauding.

"Leslie Banks ain't gonna forgive the old man that quick. The videotape still has her shaken, although she won't let on to anybody that it's still bothering her. I don't even think they're sleeping in the same room." Kory grabbed a chair and sat down.

Suddenly, a wave of nausea came over me. Every time the subject of what had happened was brought up, I would get all fucked up, because I was reminded Kory also had a thing going on with Sabrina. The images of him and her coming out of motels together, him and her fucking, and the two of them in my muthafuckin' shop with his dick all down her throat are forever etched in my mind.

Yes, I was deeply hurt. At the same time, though, her actions weren't a cause for her to be murdered by her boyfriend, Eric. She was a piece of ass, for crying out loud. Ain't no ass worth killing or dying over.

I loved Sabrina. She was my girl. As crazy as it may sound, I even miss her. She was only out to get hers. I just hate that she knew all of my business and used it to get Kory. I always knew Kory was a ho and that Sabrina carried herself like a damn prostitute. Therefore, it was really no surprise to me when they were caught on tape doing explicit things. But Phil? That's an altogether different story. Besides, Kory wasn't married to me when it all went down, so I looked at it as he wasn't cheatin' on *me*, but on Mikala.

Nobody could understand why I would go to Sabrina's funeral. Even though it was clear she had no respect for our friendship, I felt it was only right to go pay my respect to her and her family. Sure, she and Kory had fucked around, but it's not right to harbor ill will against the deceased. I lost a friend, but her mother lost a daughter. Who's suffering the bigger loss here?

To no one's surprise, Leslie did not attend Sabrina's funeral. Phil was there, though, which was a *big* surprise since Leslie kept a short leash on his ass. What was she still trippin' on Sabrina for anyway? Sabrina couldn't do any more harm. Like the saying goes, "It's not the dead you have to worry about; it's the living."

Chapter 26

Christian

"Hey Marcella, I'm about five minutes away. You can come out now," I said to her on my cell phone. Kory offered to take Kamryn with him so I could meet with Amir. I got up early and placed a call to the mayor's office to see if he had any available times in which he could meet with me. His secretary informed me that he had a 10:30 a.m. slot open, and I took it with the promise to be there on time. As I said, there was no way I was making that visit to Amir alone. I didn't trust him, and hell, I couldn't even say I trusted myself.

"Chris, you better only be five minutes away. Don't have me locking up this house and putting the alarm on when your ass is still at home in your driveway and nowhere near my home," Marcella said, knowing that I'm always late.

However, this time I really was only five minutes away. It was very important to me to keep the appointment with Amir since I knew he could be helpful in giving us the advice we needed and with seeing to it that the bitch be put in jail for killing my baby. My only worry was what "cost" would I have to "pay" for his helpfulness.

I couldn't chance fuckin' around with Amir. There was too much at stake. Amir was certainly not my type. However, at a time in my life when I viewed my own husband as weak, I met a powerful man…Amir. I was drawn to his arrogance and his ability to do what he wanted when he wanted. The fact that he ran the whole damn city didn't hurt any. I just hoped my past indiscretions with him, and my refusal now to be with him in the way he desired, wouldn't be a deciding factor in his willingness to help us.

As I pulled up, it was clear by the look on her face that Marcella was surprised with my punctuality. While waiting for her to rearrange the cars so Lance wouldn't be blocked in, I admired her. Marcella didn't look a day older than she did when we were in school. Whereas, with the dark circles under my eyes, it looked like I'd been in a fight.

By looking at her, no one would imagine Marcella was dealing with the stress of catching Lance's ass suckin' another dude's dick, the baby mama drama from Joyce concerning Casey, and the antics of Rosalita's ass when it came to Selena, Lance's love child. I made a mental note to ask her later how she managed to keep it all together while under so much stress.

"What's up wit 'cha?" Marcella asked as she got in the car. "I can't believe your ass was telling the truth about only being five minutes away." She patted me on the back as if I was a damn child.

"I told you," I said, cutting my eyes at her.

"Well, we'll be on time. That's a first."

"Shut up," I playfully snapped.

While driving, from out the corner of my eye, I saw her staring at me. She was probably wondering why I had on sunglasses when not a glimpse of sun was shining. If only she knew I was on the verge of giving up the fight and that my eyes were still red and swollen from crying last night.

I could be having a good day, and then when I would lie down to go to sleep, the tears would start. I was in so much pain from losing my son, my heart actually ached. Whenever I had these moments, I usually got out of bed as to not wake Kory.

Upon leaving the bedroom, I would tiptoe down to KJ's room, put in my Whitney Houston CD, lie in my baby's bed, and wrap myself in his sheets. Then, I would just lie there and cry. I often prayed for God to have mercy on my soul and take my life, releasing me from the unbearable pain I experienced…if Marcella only knew the battle going on within me.

"I like your hair like that, Chris," Marcella commented after a long silence.

"You do?" I questioned, looking surprised as hell that she would compliment me on my simple do of a ponytail with an added extension. *Maybe she's just trying to make me feel good.* I gave her thanks for the compliment anyway, relieved that it didn't look as bad as I thought.

After finding an empty parking space in the lot of City Hall, we entered the building and approached the elevator to take us to the second floor. I prayed Marcella didn't pick up on the nervousness I was experiencing. Dressed in a nice conservative pair of slacks and a twin set, with the second piece of the twin set tied around my neck, I exited the elevator with Marcella following on my heels.

"Hello, can I help you?" an attractive young woman sitting behind a mahogany desk asked as soon as we had exited the elevator.

I removed my sunglasses, looking the secretary in the eye, something my daddy always told me to do when speaking to people.

"Yes, I have a ten-thirty appointment with Mayor Dunkin. My name is Christian Johnson-Banks," I responded in my professional tone.

"And you are?" the young woman inquired, looking at Marcella.

"My name is Marcella Jap."

"Okay, you two can have a seat. I will let Mayor Dunkin know you're here. Please, help yourselves to refreshments," she said before switching her young ass back to Amir's office. It didn't surprise me Amir would have a "trophy" receptionist. Just as Miss P.Y.T., pretty, young, and tempting, returned to her desk and announced that Mr. Mayor would see me, Marcella's cell phone rang and she excused herself, walking into the lobby near the elevators.

Before I could rise from the chair, Amir's ass appeared from behind his office door. He was dressed in a pair of chocolate slacks, a coffee-colored silk Italian shirt, which looked more like a t-shirt, and a sports jacket with small plaid print in all shades of brown. He even had the nerve to have on a chocolate apple hat. Who ever heard of someone wearing a hat inside a damn office while at work? But, I guess when you run the city you can wear whatever it is you want.

I hadn't even reached his office and my panties were already wet. *Damn, why does he have this effect on me? Where is Marcella? I need her in here with me, which was the whole point of me bringing her.*

"Please have Mrs. Jap join us when she completes her phone call," I said to the receptionist while walking past Amir and entering his office, catching a whiff of his Joop cologne in the process. His office even smelled good. This man definitely had class.

As I looked around his office, I could feel him watching me from behind. Just as he was admiring my beauty, I was admiring the beauty of his office. The exquisite décor was the reason Kory and I chose to use the same interior decorator for Vyss. I looked at the pictures on his ivory marble desk, which were all of Tai, his wife. *How can he be such a dog with her pictures staring him right in the face? Knowing Amir, he doesn't give a fuck.*

I walked to the sitting area of his office, where he usually conducted business, and poured a bottled water from his wet bar into a glass with ice. When I turned around, I jumped, almost spilling my water, startled by his closeness behind me. A cross between Kobe Bryant and Lebron James, his sex appeal had me wanting to jump his bones. Quickly, I sat my ass down before my legs gave out from my buckling knees.

Wanting to make this meeting a quick one, I extended my hand to him so we could get it underway. We shook hands. However, the shake lingered a little longer than it should have.

"So, what can I do for you, beautiful?" he asked while taking a seat across from me.

"Mayor Dunkin…"

"Amir."

"Okay, Amir. Well, as you know, we are in the beginning stages of prosecuting the driver of the car that struck and killed my son. The lawyer you referred us to has been very optimistic about charging her with vehicular homicide. However, the defense attorney wants charges reduced to vehicular assault, which could get her less time. Since this is her first offense and her driving record is relatively clean, he believes we will need prominent individuals from the community to speak up on our behalf, which would be one reason for my visit today.

"We also need you to voice your concern about teenagers driving with too many people in the car and listening to loud music. He also said if there was a law about not talking on cell phones while driving it may help. Apparently, she'd just received a call immediately before striking Kory Jamar. We need more stop lights, stop signs, whatever…to ensure cars slow down when driving in school zones. They recorded her speed at over 45 mph in a 20 mph zone. That's ridiculous, Mayor…I mean, Amir. Kory and I are also agreeing to finally be interviewed and we would like you to be present," I stated so quickly I didn't think he understood everything I had said, although he was nodding his head as an indication that he was following me.

"Is that all you need, Christian?" he asked, as if nothing I said would be a problem.

"Yes, Amir, that's all I need," I responded quietly, feeling myself getting emotional.

"Call my receptionist and let her know when the interview is going to be and when the trial begins. I'll do anything to help your family, Christian. As for your other requests, I'll address them at the next City Council meeting."

"Thank you," I managed to say through the tears.

"I can't even begin to imagine the pain you must be feeling," Amir voiced while rolling his chair closer to me. "Therefore, I'm not going to tell you I know how you feel and that everything's going to be okay. I've said I'm sorry so many times, I feel stupid even repeating it to you now. But I will tell you if there's anything at all I can do for you or your family, don't hesitate to call."

After he handed me a few tissues from his desk, I turned my head to blow my nose and then rose from my seat to throw the tissue in the wastebasket. I thought Amir may have changed his stripes, but I guess I was sadly mistaken. No sooner than the thought had crossed my mind, he came up behind me, wrapping his arms tightly around my waist.

Where in the hell is Marcella Jap's ass?

I know I should've pushed him away, but I couldn't. I seemed to have a thing for men I couldn't have. I let him rub on me for a few seconds, and then he spun me around and kissed me dead on the lips. Now, I'm not usually one who's all into kissing because I consider it to be very intimate, and although I should've stopped him, I didn't. I actually found myself reciprocating his tongue dance.

His hands were quick. One minute, they were on my ass; the next minute, they were up my shirt, unhooking my bra. I turned my back to him in an effort to gain my composure, but all he did was caress my breasts from behind, which turned me on even more. As much as I hate to admit it, I actually leaned back into him. I hadn't felt that turned on since...hmm, since the last time I saw Amir.

"Unh-unh, Amir, I need to go," I objected while breaking the embrace and fixing my bra and shirt.

"Damn, Christian, you....just don't know." He plopped back down in his chair.

"Thanks, Amir, for agreeing to help us." I managed to fake a grin. "Kory and I really appreciate it. I will get back to your receptionist as soon as I have the interview scheduled." I extended my hand to him as he stood up, and we shook. He kissed each one of my fingers one at a time. Then, he handed me a business card.

"What's this?" I asked, giving him a twisted look since I'd already had Amir's business card from when we first met.

Before he answered, I looked down at it and saw it was a business card to Lynn Square, a place where the city houses Amir when he needs to be "alone" to work. It's sort of like his little hide-out.

Getting the message, and with nothing left to say, I approached the door as he hurried to my side, whispering in my ear that he'd be there every night after nine o'clock for the next two weeks. He gently kissed my ear and then returned to "Mayor" mode. He didn't have to spell it out. I knew very well what he was insinuating.

Once we reached the lobby area, he informed the receptionist to expect my call within the next few days. While turning to extend my final thanks, I heard Marcella's raised voice from out in the hallway near the elevators. I could only hear one side of the conversation, which meant she was still on the phone. She didn't so much as raise her head when I exited the office.

Good, she's engrossed in her conversation. That will give me some time to get my shit together before she starts with her questioning about me and Mr. Mayor's meeting.

As we exited the building, Marcella was still on the phone. How her phone managed to maintain reception while we were in the elevator was beyond me, while mine would drop a call if a hard wind blew. Since it was raining, and since I couldn't do any damage to my store-purchased hair, I agreed to walk alone to get the car.

I walked slowly to the car and drove even slower as I approached the front door of City Hall, figuring we both needed two or three minutes alone. That way, she could finish her telephone call without me being all up in her business and I could cool off without her questioning why I needed to cool off.

As I pulled up, she jumped in, shutting her phone forcibly and slamming the door so hard I thought it was going to come off the hinges. Not saying a word, she leaned her head back against the headrest and began to cry.

Now who done gone and put her panties in a bunch?

Chapter 27

Lance

I can't believe it! I didn't give two shits about Marcella being in an important meeting with the mayor. She shouldn't have been badmouthing Rosalita to Selena. Yeah, I sprung Selena up on her after five years, but Marcella's mature and I expected her to get along with Rosalita. I swear…I'm sick of them and all the bullshit.

As if her badmouthing wasn't enough, Marcella had the nerve to confront Rosalita about Selena's hair needing to be washed, and then took it upon herself to wash it when Selena came over to visit. Why would she do some shit like that, especially after I told her time and time again Rosalita did not want her to touch Selena's hair when she's over. I had to constantly remind her that she wasn't Selena's mother.

This is the same thing that happened when Casey was younger. I swear…I can't take this.

Sometimes my hate for Marcella is so strong that I just want to move somewhere she can't find me. Everybody kept telling me not to marry such a young girl, but *noooo*, I was all smitten by the attention she gave me. She appreciated the flowers, the trips, and the gifts I showered her with. We had only been dating two months before I bought her a full-length mink. My daddy taught me that's how young men should treat women. So, I kept buying her love. I should've known the first time we made love to run and never look back.

While in New York for the Broadway play *Dreamgirls*, I was so thirsty for the pussy that I let her get anything she wanted. She damn near lost her mind, picking up two and three leather coats at a time, designer clothing, purses, etc. After unloading the bellman's cart of her bags from the shopping spree into our room, we took a carriage ride through Central Park, which was the most romantic thing I'd ever done. When the ride was almost over, I jumped out of the carriage and acted like I'd fallen. That's when I went into a long speech about how she'd always been there when I was down and how she always helped me get back up. Then, to her surprise, I got on one knee and pulled out the most beautiful ring she'd ever seen, a Lolite ring from Tiffany and Co. set in platinum with a 1½ round cut center stone. Of course, she said yes and here we are today.

We married in New York and honeymooned in London, touring other places in England for two weeks before returning home. That's the day the honeymoon ended and the bullshit started.

Chapter 28

Christian

As I pulled into my driveway, I pressed the garage door opener. Nothing. I pushed it again and it still didn't open. *Damnit!* I put the car in park and got out to manually key in the code for the garage to open.

Pissed would've been an understatement for how I was feeling. I had asked Kory more times than I could count to call the company and have it fixed. I knew he had been busy with the new shop, but hell, it wouldn't take any time to pick up the phone, dial some numbers, and set up an appointment. I even asked him for the telephone number so I could call the place my damn self, but he kept saying he'd take care of it. He did something to it the other day and it was working for a while, but now it was broken again.

While the garage door began to rise, it came off the track. I quickly pressed the code again to stop it from making the horrible noise like it was going to fall off the hinges. Now, I'm royally pissed and I whipped out my cell phone to place a call to his inconsiderate ass.

"What's up?" he answered on the first ring.

"Kory, did you call the man about the garage?" I asked in an infuriated tone.

"I'm going to call right now."

"No, you're not! You've been saying that! You know I don't have time to fool with this garage door, especially if the media is waiting outside like vultures," I screamed as I walked into the house. "Give me the number and I'll call them."

"Chris, calm down. I will call the man when I get home. Damn!"

Oh no, this nigga didn't just get foxy with me, did he? I actually had to take the phone away from my ear and look at it.

"Forget it, Kory. I'll look the number up myself. You just better hope you get home before he gets here, 'cause I just might change the code on your muthafuckin' ass." I slammed the phone down, not giving him the chance to say anything. I was fed up with his ass.

It took me over twenty minutes to locate the number; it took another hour for the guy to come out; and it took another two hours for him to fix it. All the while, Mr. Kory Jamar Banks, Sr. hadn't surfaced.

Once the issue of the broken garage door had been resolved, I slipped into a hot, papaya oil bath. The tub's jet stream made me feel like I was at the spa.

After stepping out of the tub, I slapped a little gel in my hair to make it lay right, and then proceeded to search through all three of my closets at least five times before pulling out a sexy pair of Seven Jeans and an off-the-shoulder black top with rhinestones spelling out *Dangerous* across the bosom area.

Once I finished dressing, I slid on my new Chanel toe ring, admiring the way it looked on my freshly pedicured toe. I then put on my new pair of bad ass sandals that laced up my legs and had butterflies made out of rhinestones on them. I accessorized with a silver chain belt and a Tiffany's choker. Grabbing my black Chanel bag, I started to transfer the contents from the purse I had carried earlier into it.

I sprayed some Heavenly on extra thick and in all the right places, and applied bronzer to give me a more glamorous look. I painted my lips with my favorite lip gloss, giving my lips a shine that would make a nigga want to suck the color outta them, and threw on my tinted glasses to complete the look.

After checking myself out in the mirror, I placed my wedding ring inside the side compartment of my purse and sashayed my tail out the side door.

As I backed out of the driveway, I made sure I punched in a new code for the garage opener. "I told you I'd fix ya ass, Mr. Banks!"

I entered Lynn Square into my navigational system, threw in my D'Angelo CD, and turned it up full blast.

I want some of that brown suga, alright!!!

Chapter 29

Christian

Kory had been blowing up my cell phone. He must have arrived home shortly after I left and was mad as hell that he couldn't get in the garage without the code. He must've thought I was playing with ass. Oh no, baby, game time was over.

I dialed into my voicemail to listen to his most recent message.

"Chris, I know your phone is on, and I know you see my name on the caller ID. As much as we've been through lately, I can't believe you're not answering the phone and that you would go and change the code on me. Call when you get this message."

No sooner had I finished listening to his message, he was ringing my phone again. I would've turned my phone off, but I was afraid there'd be an emergency of some kind and no one would be able to get in touch with me. Therefore, I just politely pressed the ignore button and kept riding for the remaining fifteen minutes it took me to reach downtown Detroit.

After finally arriving at my destination, I pulled my car up to the valet and handed him the key. When I tried to tip him the neatly folded ten-dollar bill, he refused, telling me it had already been taken care of. I'm sure I had Amir to thank.

Before exiting my truck, I checked myself in the mirror one last time, gave myself a squirt of Heavenly, and applied a fresh coat of lip gloss. As I approached the entrance to Lynn Square, I glanced around at the surroundings. It was really nice.

Wow, the luxuries of having money and power...and an abundance of it.

Walking into the awaiting elevator, I informed the attendant that I had a meeting with Mayor Dunkin. He pressed a button in the elevator and Amir answered through the intercom system. The attendant announced my name and Amir pressed a button, allowing us access to the third floor foyer where I was supposed to meet him at the bar. When the door opened, the attendant escorted me out of the elevator and pointed me in the direction of the bar's entrance. No one was in the bar except Amir and a few waiters, servers, and bartenders.

After removing my frames, I took in the décor. I had never seen any shit like it. There were no walls, just mahogany-tinted glass everywhere. The lights gave the bar an orange glow. The bar stretched from one end of the room to the other, and it was made of the same glass the walls were made of. To my astonishment, the floor looked like it was made of glass, too, and had me almost scared to walk on it. I found myself literally tiptoeing across to the other side of the room where Amir was sitting.

As I approached the table, Amir stood and reached out for my hand, kissing it. After taking my seat, I noticed he'd already taken the liberty of ordering red wine. I lifted my glass to take a sip, but Amir gently grabbed my hand to stop me, saying he wanted to make a toast.

"From a man who has almost everything he wants, to a woman who's missing something," he said.

Oh shit, what am I doing here? I thought to myself as we tapped glasses, sensing I had entered a danger zone.

Amir and I sat there talking about everything. Soon, the subject touched on our significant others. He went into great detail about when he met Tai and how he thought she was the prettiest woman he'd ever laid eyes on. They met in college, although they attended different universities and were introduced at the Southern Classic by a mutual friend. She graduated a year before him, and a year after he graduated, they were married. The more he spoke of his wife, the more his face lit up.

"Damn, Amir, you really love her, don't you?" I asked, almost in a jealous tone.

"Christian, I breathe my wife. She's smart, beautiful, and she handles her business. I think I've loved her since the first day I met her," he responded, grinning broadly.

"It's funny you should say that because that's the way it was with me and Kory. The first day I saw him, I was head over heels in love. I thought he was the finest man I had ever seen."

"You know Banks is still head over heels in love with you, don't you?" Amir asked, taking a sip of his wine.

"And just how do you know that, Mr. Mayor?" I said seductively.

"Everybody knows the story of Mr. and Mrs. Banks. We know he left his first wife for you. We know you gave him the child she couldn't...no disrespect intended."

"None taken. What else does everybody *think* they know about me?"

"We also know you got a little bit of game with you. You're aware Doug and I are boys, right? As a matter of fact, I just talked to him the other day and he asked about you."

Damn! Now he's really got my attention. "And?"

"And what?" he asked, knowing damn well what I was talking about.

"What did you tell him?" I said, leaning forward in my seat.

"I told him about the case and how I had been working on helping your family get stoplights and new crossing guards and the likes."

"Doug is a good man," I said, sounding full of regret, while leaning back in my chair and starting to reminisce.

"You didn't seem to think so when he was inhaling every ounce of you. That dude was strung out. I don't know if it was his pride or what, but he took the breakup very hard."

"Amir, Doug came into my life during the worst time. Actually, I was competing with Mikala to win Kory's love. I couldn't see Doug for the man he was. He deserved much better than what I could offer at the time. I hate to admit it, but I used Doug to get attention from Kory. In the process of dating him, I began to care for him a lot. It scared me, though. I thought if I started caring about Doug too deeply, I'd lose Kory forever. So, I made myself distant from him."

Amir looked at me for a minute before speaking. "Then that scenario went down at the shop that landed my man Banks in the county jail."

"How did you know about that?" I said, now starting to worry about what other shit he knew about me.

"How do you think he got out?"

"He...he told me his sister posted bail," I said while stuttering, not sure of where this conversation was going.

"Yeah, Marcella posted the bail...with *my* money. I went down there and paid it, but she signed her name on the line." I sat there looking like a damn deer caught in headlights, eyes wide as hell. "Why would Kory tell me Marcella was the one who bailed him out?"

"Because Banks didn't want everybody in his business, and he knew if Marcella would've gotten the money from her dude, he would have been asking questions. Don't worry, though. Banks doesn't owe me any money or nothing like that. He paid it back as soon as he was released."

"I guess I should thank you, even though I wouldn't have at the time." I shook my head in total disbelief. "Why has Kory been lying all this time about it when he could've just told me the truth?"

"Christian, it's no big deal. Everyone has secrets they keep from their mate. I'm sure you won't run home and tell Banks you were sitting in the bar of Lynn Square's third floor foyer with Amir Dunkin."

He has a point there. Amir's damn right I won't be telling Kory shit.

"Yeah, you're right," I whispered. It just seemed to me that what Kory lied about was so stupid. Where as, telling him about my date with Amir would get me fucked up.

"Kory never told me what happened, but Doug did. He said some woman named Sabrina answered your cell phone and gave him all the goods."

"Damn, you know about Sabrina?" My mouth dropped wide open. *Is there anything this man doesn't know?*

"I don't know too much about her, but I do hope you're not still friends with her after she pulled a stunt like that."

Well, he doesn't know as much as I thought he did. So, I spent the next hour telling him all about her and Eric while indulging in several more glasses of red wine. After I finished, Amir went on to tell me about the time Tai cheated on him.

"Tai! Are you trying to tell me your wife, Tai Dunkin, stepped out on you, Mr. Mayor?" His words were shocking to me.

"Tai knew I had been getting around on her while we were in college, but she thought I'd stop once we got married."

"Why do women think that?" I questioned him as if he knew the answer.

"Hell if I know."

"So tell me something, Mr. Mayor. Why? Why do men cheat?"

"Hold up now, beautiful. It's not just us men doing the cheating. But I can't answer because I don't have the answer. My wife asked me the same thing."

"And what did you tell her?"

"The same thing I'm telling you...I don't know why. The incident that sent Tai over the edge was when a woman from Atlanta came to our house and told my wife, right to her face, that she was six weeks pregnant with my child. This was right after I put my bid in to run for mayor. The woman threatened to blow my shit out of the water if we didn't give her ten thousand dollars right then and there."

"What did Tai do? What did the woman do? Do you have a child with her?" I inquired, now sitting on the edge of my seat.

"First of all, no, I don't have a child with her. It turned out she was unsure of who the father was. Therefore, she decided not to go public, for fear of embarrassing herself and ruining her career with the Fulton County Board of Education if in fact the child turned out not to be mine. She ended up having an abortion, which I gladly paid for just to be rid of her ass."

"You're one lucky nigga."

"You're right. I did luck out with that one. However, I'm not that lucky, though. Shortly after it was resolved, Tai started doing her thing. I knew she wanted to leave me, but she was too embarrassed. She didn't want to face people and give them the chance to say, 'I told you so'."

"I know what that feels like," I responded while nodding my head.

"The next thing I knew, she started fixing herself up all nice and staying out late. I suspected she was creeping around, but I didn't care. It just gave me more time to do me."

"Did you confront her?"

"Oh yeah, plenty of times. She denied it for about a year. Then she got bold on a nigga and told me the truth. She'd met some managing engineer for GM and they'd been hanging out for a while."

"What did you say?" I asked, barely able to control myself.

"There wasn't much I could say. Tai's grown, just as I am, and she'll do what she wants to do. It's inevitable that one of us will leave after my term as mayor has expired."

I sat there speechless. I knew Amir did his dirt and all, but I had no idea he was getting a prescription of his own medicine... and worse yet, that Tai was the one filling it.

"You love Banks, don't you?" he asked me out of the blue.

"Why do you ask?"

"I just wanted to see how you'd reply. I already know the answer. You're a lot like Tai. You've been hurt in a deep place, and no one has ever been able to mend that pain."

"You're a very smart man, Mr. Mayor. And to answer your question...yes, I do. I love my husband very much."

"Then why do you wish to divorce him?"

"How do you know every damn thing?"

"I'm Mr. Mayor," he answered smugly.

"I don't know. I'm so confused right now. I wanted Kory so badly until I got him. Then I found out he wasn't all that I had made him out to be. It turned from loving him to needing to win him. Once the game was over and I was crowned the winner, the thrill was gone." I paused to take a sip from my glass and gather my thoughts before continuing.

"Then at other times, I find myself loving Kory so much that it scares me. Sometimes I think I'm obsessed with him. I painted a picture in my mind of living a perfect life with a perfect husband and perfect kids. When things didn't turn out as such, I wanted to put all the blame on him. Am I making any sense to you?"

"You're making a lot of sense. You love Kory. He's perfect to you. But when he does things less than perfect, it taints the image, and you waver about whether or not you want to be with the less-than-perfect version of your husband."

"You're *real* good, Amir."

"Thank you," he said in his deep, sexy voice.

Suddenly, I felt bad for ignoring Kory's calls and not giving him the new code to the garage opener. Hell, I should've been at home fixing him dinner and reading Kamryn a bedtime story instead of sitting with the mayor getting smashed. Amir was right. I put too much pressure on Kory. As Amir and I sat in silence, I listened to Mariah Carey's "I Don't Want to Cry" playing in the background. The song seemed so fitting for the thoughts running through my head.

"Go home, Christian. Try to make it work with Banks," Amir said, as if reading my mind. "He loves you, and you obviously love him. Don't get stuck in a rut like me and Tai, not knowing how to get out. Try counseling again, if you think you both need it. Go on vacation. Buy a new house. Move away. Have another baby. Do whatever it takes to reconnect with him."

"Amir, can I ask you a question? Why are you so interested in what Kory and I do?" I asked quickly, not giving him the opportunity to say whether I could ask or not.

"In my eyes, the two of you are perfect for one another. If any two people deserve a little bit of happiness, it's you two. You've both messed up from time to time, but have been able to find your way back to each other every time. Neither of you are going anywhere. From the hell I heard you gave Mikala, you won't let anybody else have him anyway. And from the police report about...you know who, he's not letting you run off with anyone else, either. Soooo..."

As I stood to straighten myself out, Amir also stood and began walking me to the elevator.

"I had plans of getting you drunk and taking advantage of you. You know that, right?" he said, smiling.
"And I had plans on you taking complete advantage of me," I replied.

Leaning down, Amir gave me a sweet but quick peck on the cheek. That time, however, his presence didn't give me the butterflies. Instead, I felt a sort of inner peace.

"Yes, this is Mayor Dunkin. I have a guest leaving from the third floor foyer," Amir announced into the elevator's intercom system.

Chapter 30

Christian

By the time I got home, Kory was already asleep. I wanted to wake him up to talk, but thought better of it. I had already been selfish enough for the evening. I noticed the Wendy's Hamburger wrappers in the trash and was instantly saddened. A man who worked so hard at trying to keep me happy should've had a hot meal waiting for him on the table when he came in the door.

After checking on Kamryn, who was sleeping peacefully, I walked into the bathroom, took a quick shower, put on my pajamas, not bothering to tie my hair up, and walked into KJ's room. As soon as I entered his room, I walked over to the window and opened it to rid the room of its stuffiness. Once I was settled under the blankets of KJ's bed, I hit the power button for the TV and VCR.

I guess I fell asleep watching the tape of KJ's 5th birthday party, because when I woke up, the television had a black screen, indicating the tape had reached its end. Pulling myself out of his bed, I powered off the TV and VCR, quietly checked on Kamryn, who was still sleeping, and then entered my bedroom…where a big fight awaited me.

"Where the fuck was you last night?"

"Kory, don't start with me, please." As I brushed past him to go in the bathroom to brush my teeth and wash my face, his ass followed closely on my heels.

"Answer my question, Christian," he demanded in a tone I guess was supposed to scare me.

Not frightened in the least, I looked at him with a mouthful of toothpaste and shook my head, signaling for him to leave me alone.

"Answer me, damnit!" Kory shouted while grabbing my arm.

"You better get the fuck out my face," I said calmly after I had rinsed my mouth.

Storming away, he went and plopped down on the edge of the bed. Strolling nonchalantly from the bathroom and past him to the nightstand, I picked up the phone and dialed Marcella's number.

"Mar, can you come pick Kam up and watch her for a few hours while I go to the hairdresser?" I asked.

"I'm actually right around the corner from your house, so I can come and get her right now."

After hanging up, I went and woke Kamryn up, leaving a fuming Kory still sitting in the same spot on the bed. I quickly washed Kamryn up in the sink, dressed her, and headed downstairs as Marcella blew her horn.

When I ran outside in my bare feet, she inched up in the driveway like she was going to hit me, and we both laughed. Marcella took Kamryn from my arms, strapped her in the backseat, and backed out of the driveway like she was in a hurry, while I stood there waving.

When I turned to go back into the house, I tried to gather my thoughts because I knew Kory wasn't going to let the issue rest. And I was right. As soon as I walked into the bedroom, he started up again.

"Christian, I ain't gonna keep asking you the same question over again. Where the fuck was you last night?"

"Kory, let it go. I slept in KJ's room. I was watching his birthday party tape and fell asleep."

We stood in the middle of the bedroom floor, facing off with one another.

"Whatever, Christian. Where were you when we got home? You weren't in KJ's room then."

"I was out. You go out and I don't say shit. Where the fuck was you when I asked you about the garage door?"

"We ain't talking about me."

"Oh well, I guess we ain't talking then."

"When I got home, I could smell perfume and shit. You got dressed and kicked it, huh? And don't lie and say you were with Marcella because I checked with her already."

"So now you're checking up on me?" I asked while snapping my neck. "Did I say I was with Marcella? Did I say I was with anybody?" I retorted.

"You ain't said shit!" he yelled.

By this time, I had pulled out a cute sweatsuit and started to dress.

"Where are you running off to now?"

"Kory, Kamryn just left. You ain't got any more kids up in this bitch. I come and go as I damn well please. You do you…and I'll do me," I said before strolling off into the vanity room to start putting my make-up on. As I applied my lip gloss, he knocked it from my hand.

"I want some answers. You ain't goin' anywhere until you tell me what it is that I want to know!"

"First of all, I ain't a fuckin' child, Kory! But if you must know, I'm going to go get my hair cut," I said while pushing past him and walking back into our master bedroom.

"It's another nigga, ain't it? You were with another nigga, weren't you?"

His words fucked me up and caused me to stop dead in my tracks. I looked over my shoulder at him, glaring for a few seconds. "Only the guilty accuse, Kory. Maybe I should be asking you if it's another bitch."

"My son ain't even warm in the ground and your ass is out being a ho."

In a blind rage, I grabbed the lamp from the nightstand and threw it at his ass.

"You got a lot of damn nerve, and I mean a *whole* lot of nerve! When I was pregnant with your son, you were out hoeing. Remember? Matter of fact, you were cheating when you made your son. You were married, remember? You and your nasty ass daddy are part of the reason why Sabrina is dead now. Remember the tape of you sitting at my station with your fuckin' dick all down her throat? Remember that shit, Kory?

"You also don't think I know about you fucking with Bethany Samoth from the old shop. But I do, nigga. I just never said shit. So while you're ready to kick my ass about some shit you've fabricated in your mind, think about the shit you've done and are probably still doing. And know this for a fact...if you *ever* put your fuckin' hands on me again, I will have your ass locked up so quick that Amir won't be able to bail you out this time. Didn't think I knew about that shit either, did you? But I do!"

Kory stood in silence, rubbing his shoulder where the lamp had hit him.

"Yeah, what's wrong, Kory?" I asked, getting all up in his face. "You ain't got shit to say, huh? What's wrong? Which pussycat got your tongue this time?"

As he came at me like he was going to hit me, I started swinging on him in defense, breaking a nail in the process. With the back of his hand, he knocked me to the floor. Although it didn't hurt one bit, I started crying and performing like he'd shot me or something. I was throwing my arms all about and holding my head, acting like a true drama queen. I could've easily won an Academy Award for my performance.

"I'm calling the police, muthafucka!" I yelled while still on the floor, pretending to be hurt.

The next thing I knew, my cordless phone hit me in the lip. And let me tell you, that shit *did* hurt.

"Call them then, bitch!"

He stood over me, waiting for me to call. I was stuck between a rock and a hard place. If I called, they would take

Dangerously

his ass back to jail. If I didn't, I'd never be able to use that threat as leverage again.

"Stop staring at me, nigga, and get me a cold rag for my lip," I said while looking up at him from the floor.

As he walked away, I pulled myself from the floor and sat down at the foot of the bed.

"I didn't mean to bust your lip with the phone, Chris," he said dryly when he returned with a wet towel, staring at me with those beautiful brown eyes.

I rolled my eyes at him.

"You need some ice?" he asked, concerned.

"Yeah," I responded, still trying to sound mad.

When he got back with the ice, I wrapped it in the towel and applied pressure to my lip, hoping it wouldn't swell. Not wanting to fight anymore, I decided it was time to tell Kory the truth.

"Kory, there is no other man. I was mad at you for not coming home and seeing about the garage door. To get back at you, I got dressed and went out for a little while. When I came home, I was still wired up. So instead of coming into the bedroom and waking you, I went in KJ's room. I guess I was more tired than I thought and fell asleep. That's it. End of story."

Okay, so I didn't tell him the whole *truth.*

We sat on the bed next to each other in silence for a few minutes before Kory spoke. "You're right. When you told me about the garage, I should've brought my sorry ass home and saw to it that it got fixed."

"Why didn't you then?" I whispered.

"'Cuz I'm a sorry son of a bitch, that's why. I do shit I don't even think about until you go off on me. And for the record, there is no other woman."

Again, we sat in silence. Then, I reached around and hugged him. His admitting that he was wrong was good enough for me. Next thing I knew, I was playing in his hair and one thing led to another. Suddenly, my lip didn't hurt as much anymore, especially when he started planting little kisses on it.

With him not being fully dressed, there wasn't much for him to come out of, and I was out of my sweatsuit in a New York minute. Yanking my hair, he threw me into the wall and started pounding me from behind. With each thrust, I could actually hear my body hitting the wall.

In one swift movement, he swung me around and bent me over the bed. The intensity of the pain felt as if my asshole was being ripped wide open, and I was certain I would pass out.

"OOOhhhhhhhh!" I screamed with tear-filled eyes. "Kory! Stop!" I yelled in pain.

He was acting possessed and giving me the ass fucking of my life. When he finally pulled out, after spilling his seed up in me, I felt a huge relief of pressure. Still, I couldn't walk. Hell, I could hardly stand. I managed to turn around, looking at the satisfied look upon his face.

"Damn, that was good, babe," he said, grinning.

"To who, nigga?" I responded while trying to crawl to the bathroom.

Jumping up, he ran to the tub to start the water. For the next hour, we soaked together and talked. Afterwards, I applied some Preparation H to my ass, which helped to relieve some of the pain, and made sure to put the tube in my purse. I got dressed again for the second time that day, and by then, I was extremely late for my hair appointment. I prayed my hairdresser would still take me.

"Chris, you gonna give me the code or not?" Kory called out as I walked into the garage.

"Nine, six, seventy-five," I yelled, still upset over his excessive roughness.

"I'll see you at the shop. I have to stop by Karen's for a minute, and then pick up the nameplates from Office Max."

"Okay," I responded while trying to ease into a sitting position behind the steering wheel. I had no idea how I would sit long enough to get my hair done.

The things one will do for the one they love.

Chapter 31

Marcella

When we arrived at the courthouse, there were large crowds of people and media everywhere. It was so bad that the police had to escort us into the building. People were shouting obscenities at the girl who had hit KJ, and yelling at Kory and Christian that they were unfit parents. Unfazed, we walked past the crowds with our heads held high.

There were a lot of people who came out to support our family, such as Momma, Daddy, Mel, Karen, Davy, Lance, and Brandi who came in from out of town. The mayor and his wife were there, as well. The case had caused a big buzz. Even the local politicians had been making comments about it on T.V.

"Young drivers with several passengers are the leading cause of fatalities in the state, and something has to be done. We are strongly considering raising the age limit of drivers from sixteen to eighteen," Mayor Dunkin said to the news media as he and his wife entered the filled-to-capacity courtroom.

As everyone took their seats, I wondered why the courtroom wasn't closed to the public. Still, the judge would not let the media into the courtroom because the girl being charged was a minor. Her name was withheld from the press. The newspapers simply referred to her as the "Underage Driver." I wanted to call the media and tell them if she's old enough to get behind the wheel of a car, then she's old enough to have her name printed so everyone will know who the teenager was that hit and killed my nephew.

Her name is Amy Stoot, and she was crying and performing all in the courtroom. I guess she feared her life would be snatched away from her just like my nephew's. Her mother held onto her for dear life. By the possessed look on Christian's face and the way she kept balling up her fists, I feared she was going to go over and fuck both of them up. She stared at Amy so hard, not blinking once to my knowledge.

Amy's mother noticed Christian staring in their direction, but knew better than to come over and say anything after the scene at the hospital. I don't know why her mother allowed Amy to bring her young ass to the hospital anyway. Amy should've known nobody was going to be happy to see her. She would've been better off just calling on the phone to find out what happened to KJ. But *no*, her entire family showed up, and it almost resulted in a riot right there in the emergency room's waiting area. Christian lunged at Amy, and would've toppled her if Mel hadn't jumped in the way. I know Christian, and I know she would've killed Amy if she had gotten a hold of her.

As the trial got underway, my eyes filled with tears while listening to the judge read the reports of what happened the day of KJ's death. The whole time the judge was talking, Mrs.

Stoot, Amy's mother, never took her eyes off Christian. I guess she wanted to be prepared just in case Christian tried to jump on her daughter again.

The judge cleared his throat before he began speaking. "On April 14th, Amy Stoot's 1998 Chevy Cavalier struck and killed Kory Banks, Jr. as he walked across the street on Highway 98. Amy did not stop after she struck Kory. Amy, with your plea, you are facing manslaughter and hit and run charges. If found guilty, you could serve the maximum time held in the youth detention home until you're twenty-one years of age. The minimum sentence is three years probation."

After the judge finished, Amy's lawyer put in a plea of No Contest. So the judge set another trial date for July 3rd, the day before KJ's birthday. *Damn, that's gonna be hell on all of us.*

Before court was adjourned, the judge also stated Amy's driving privileges were suspended until after the case was over. *Hell, the damage had already been done.*

Chapter 32

Christian

"Christian, would you hurry up?"

I silently prayed for Kory to quit calling my name. I was moving as fast as I could. Shit, he was the one who let me oversleep, knowing I had to go to my hair appointment, pick my suit up from the tailor and his from the cleaners, drop off my dad's suit to him, and take Kamryn to the sitter's. On top of all that, the phone had been ringing like crazy. But did he think about any of that while he was standing at the bottom of the stairs hollering my name? Hell no!

The grand opening of Vyss was an invitation-only event, so I didn't have to worry about seeing too many insignificant people who I didn't give a damn about. My only worries were hoping that the caterers and the Jazz band would be there on time. I knew the reporters were going to be punctual if for nothing else than to be nosy.

"Chrissssss, hurry up!"

I scurried around the bedroom in search of my other shoe. I couldn't imagine where in the hell it had went between when I had snuck them in here so Kory wouldn't see them until now. There was no way I could ask him to help me find the missing shoe. Then he would have known I bought new ones after I specifically told him not to go buy new white gators to match his suit when he already had some from our wedding he had only worn once.

My suit was sharp, as they say. The jacket was low cut, and I had my *girls* hanging all out with the help of a Miracle Bra, compliments of Victoria's Secrets. My slacks stopped a little above the ankle and were cuffed, and the shoes were what really set the outfit off. So, there was no way in hell I was steppin' out without my new shoes on.

"Babe, what are you doing?" Kory asked while entering the room.

Before I could answer, he surveyed my closet and shook his head. Shit was thrown everywhere. As I looked up from the closet floor, I noticed he was wearing a new pair of shoes, the same ones we had argued about for twenty minutes when we were at the mall two weeks ago. I couldn't believe it. *The whole time, I'd been trying to hide* my *new shoes from him and here his ass went and bought those damn shoes.* Wanting to keep the peace, I decided not to say shit.

After disappearing into the bathroom to check his appearance in the mirror, he emerged holding my shoe in his hand like it was Cinderella's glass slipper. I couldn't help but laugh and wonder how in the hell it had gotten all the way in the bathroom. I thought Kory was going to fuss, but he didn't. He probably figured I noticed his damn shoes, and therefore, he wouldn't have much room to talk about my needless spending.

During the ride, we talked about our plans for the new shop. I found it hard to keep my eyes off him, trying hard to suppress the overwhelming desire to eat his ass up. Failing to control my urge, I leaned over, unzipped his pants, and attempted to give him my lil' rendition of Downtown Julie Brown. Unfortunately, he lightly pushed my head back, expressing he didn't want to get my MAC lip color all over his brand new suit. I couldn't be pissed at the rejection because I felt exactly where he was coming from. Still, I was fiendin' for him.

After arriving at the shop, Kory dropped me off in front while he parked the truck. I couldn't believe how many people were already there. Everyone who was anyone in the city, and who had been invited, was there.

When we walked in, I heard the Jazz band playing, which made me happy, and I spotted the servers walking around with appetizers. My anxiety level dropped considerably upon learning the DJ and caterers were on their jobs. Once inside the foyer, we spotted Amir and Tai, who were there to show their support. Kory went off to talk to some people he'd invited, which gave Amir the go-ahead to come over and talk with me. All of a sudden, I started feeling nauseous. As Amir approached, I hurried off in the opposite direction before he could reach me. Not discouraged, he came right over to the table where I was standing.

"Kory Banks is one lu-cky man," he said with a devilish look on his face.

"Thank you," I responded, nodding my head to acknowledge his correctness.

"How you doing, Christian?" he asked, as if he was genuinely concerned with my well being.

"Fine."

"Shit, I can see that. You damn sure are fine."

I tried to look away, avoiding eye contact with him. Just as I was served a ginger ale and turned to walk away from Amir, up walks Doug, looking fine as hell. I'd never thought of Doug as fine...maybe nice looking, but not fine. However, that night was a different muthafuckin' night. It must've been the money making him so appealing, same as with Amir. Doug exchanged dap with Amir, and then gave me a hug and a kiss on the cheek, his lips lingering a little longer than they should have.

"This is some party you threw, Christian," Doug said while looking me directly in the eyes.

"Thanks. We wanted it to be something special. So, how is married life treating you?" I asked while my eyes darted around the room.

"It's cool," he replied dryly.

As my eyes searched the room for Kory, I spotted my cousins Rayna, Randel, Raylisa, Royce, and Ravonna, who I hadn't seen since KJ's funeral. I figured my daddy must've invited them. While easing through the crowd, and while trying not to get my feet stepped on since they were killing me from my new shoes, I noticed Leslie Banks over in a corner talking to Mikala. Words couldn't describe my hatred for them, and I questioned why Mikala was even there.

As I walked past, acting as if I didn't see them, Mikala had the nerve to grab me by the arm of my new fucking suit. I turned around so quick that I caught a sharp pain in my neck. I just knew the bitch wasn't toughing me.

"Christian, I just wanted to thank you for inviting me. There are so many people here that Mama Lez has been introducing me to."

She went on for another minute or so, but I had tuned her out by then. First of all, I was wondering where she got the warped idea *I* had invited her. *Me* invite *Mikala*? That didn't even sound right. I was happy when Leslie started talking to her again so I could politely make my way in a totally different direction. With all the reporters present, I sure as hell didn't want to end up in a picture with Mikala's whack ass, or better yet, have them snap a picture of me *kicking* her ass.

As I headed towards my cousins, Kory stopped me for pictures. I stood there posing with him and gave statements to the press. My feet were killing me, I felt like I had to throw up, and the last thing I wanted to do was take pictures. But hey, I had to be the cordial hostess, right?

As I got closer to Rayna, I started smiling immediately. Rayna is the only one out of Whit's kids that actually did something with her life. She's the one who I used to be the closest to. I walked over and we hugged for what seemed like forever, both crying upon contact. She looked good, too. The girl always had a shape. Her hair, which hung a little below her shoulders, was reddish brown with strawberry blonde streaks. She had on a periwinkle cocktail dress, and her matching shoes were sharp as hell. The Air Force was doing something right by her. When Rayna caught me checking out her left hand, which had a rock on it damn near as big as mine, she grabbed my hand and pulled me down to sit next to her. She couldn't stop grinning as she told me all about Mr. Wonderful a.k.a. Dirk Loxx. Hell, she didn't have to sell me on him. I already liked him. Shit, his name was sexy as hell to me, so I'm sure his body would get my approval.

One by one, Rayna's siblings returned to the table and brought me up to date with what had been going on with them. Raylisa was out on parole and had just given birth to another baby. She'd regained custody of her other two children in May and was working as a clerk at a local library.

Randel had finally married his longtime girlfriend, Jasmine. The two of them together had about as much common sense as Kamryn. They were doing okay by their standards. She was recently promoted to manager of Payless Shoes and he was working as a waiter at TGIF. I wanted to slap both of them with a bit of ambition, but instead kept my comments to a minimum. Randel turned out to be nice looking, with the exception of his crooked and decaying teeth. Jasmine was smiling like she really had a prize. Hey, if she liked it, I loved it.

Royce told me he was still on crack, but not a crackhead. He thinks since he goes to work everyday driving a taxi in the city, he's not an addict. Hell if he wasn't. I was suddenly glad

I had locked my purse in the safe, because I didn't trust Royce as far as I could throw him. Hell, he looked worse than Gator from Jungle Fever, and he had an unbelievable stench with him, too. Lord, help him.

Ravonna, the youngest of Whit's children, was doing okay. Right now, she's taking classes at the local college to become a dental tech. Lawd, she changes career choices like she changes her drawers…which I hope is often. At KJ's funeral, she expressed an interest in becoming a mortician. Before that, she was in cosmetology school. Then, she talked about becoming an E-Bay seller. I swear that girl's got Whit's hustle in her if she doesn't have anything else.

I excused myself from their table, giving each of them a business card and telling them to call me anytime. I figured if the damn Banks family could call our house in the middle of the goddamn night to talk about absolutely nothing, then why shouldn't the Johnson's?

I stopped and talked to Kory for a second, then chatted with Tanisha and her flavor of the day. She told me how Greg, that day's flavor, was letting her brothers rent his house, which was right around the cul-de-sac from my home. Immediately, I sensed that Tanisha was only dealing with him for his loot. I mean, the white boy is fine and all, but he ain't her type.

After chit-chatting with them for a few moments more, I excused myself to go speak to my daddy. However, my feet were hurting *so* bad, I ended up hobbling into my office instead, closing the door behind me. As I plopped down on the sofa, I kicked off those damn shoes, cursed them, and then started massaging my feet. After about ten seconds, the pain subsided. Looking over, I picked up a picture from the end table of KJ sitting in Kory's chair, getting his first hair cut. After returning the picture to its place, I hobbled over to my locker and took out a photo album. I flipped through the pictures of KJ with Santa Claus at the mall, his first day of kindergarten, KJ holding Alexis and Kamryn when they were first born, and pictures of them at the swimming pool. Suddenly, the dam burst and I began to drown in my tears. I missed my son something terribly. As I looked at the pictures, all I could see was a miniature version of Kory, Sr. KJ's face was the exact face of his father, the face I fell so deeply in love with close to ten years ago.

Instantly, I felt guilty about being able to celebrate anything without KJ here with us.

How can I smile? How can I be laughing it up when I'm crying on the inside? How can I continue on with this facade?

Then the thoughts of taking my own life returned.

God, please, hit me with some incurable disease, let me get run over by a car or into an accident where I just die at the scene. Let me have a massive heart attack and drop dead or eat something poisonous. Anything, God...just please take me. I'm begging you. Don't leave me here. I can't take it. I'm not strong enough.

By now, I was hysterically rocking back and forth on the couch. I couldn't breathe, and it felt like a clamp was squeezing my chest walls. I needed air. I opened the window, stuck my head out, and kept it there for a few minutes until I somewhat calmed down.

Returning to the sofa, I grabbed up the framed picture of KJ again from the end table and held it so tight that the frame and glass broke, cutting my palms and fingers. A fleeting thought of using the fragments of glass to cut my wrist crossed my mind, but I was too scared. I rinsed my hands in the office bathroom's sink, poured peroxide over them, which hurt like hell, and lay down on the couch, closing my eyes for what I thought was a minute. The next thing I knew, Kory entered.

"Babe, why are you laying down? Are you ready to go home? And what happened to your hands?"

Before I could answer, he surveyed the room and saw what I'd been up to. Sitting on the edge of the couch, he cupped my face with both of his hands.

"Babe, why didn't you tell me? Why didn't you come and get me? I would've taken you home. Heather and Maurice can close up around here. Besides, it's almost over anyway."

I lifted my head to look at him, and as I opened my mouth to tell him I was ready to go, shit I had eaten two weeks ago came flying out. I rushed to our office bathroom, fell to my knees, and prayed to the porcelain God. *Damn, I hate vomiting.* I must have stayed on the floor for twenty minutes, with Kory standing behind me and rubbing my back.

When there was nothing left to come out, I flushed the toilet. As I looked down at my suit, which was ruined, Kory walked over and retrieved a jogging suit from my locker. He helped me change before summoning the custodian into the office to clean up the mess. Kory then told me he was going to get the truck and pull it up to the back door so I wouldn't have to walk far. With everyone to the front of the shop, I left undetected.

After Kory carefully helped me inside the truck, I laid my head against the window and started to bawl. He handed me tissues from the glove compartment and told me it was okay to cry. As he pulled away, he inserted my Whitney Houston CD, and we both sang along.

And I...will always love you, you ooh ohh ooh, I'll always love you.

Chapter 33

Marcella

The last couple weeks my mother seemed tired. She complained of shortness of breath and body aches. Leslie called to tell me that when she woke up this morning, she only had enough strength to make breakfast, read the paper, and make one phone call. After doing just that little bit, she was too exhausted to do anything else and returned to bed to get some rest.

When she went to the doctor for her yearly examination a few months back, she didn't say anything was the matter with her, so I figured her fatigue was the result of all the stress she had experienced over the last year dealing with KJ's death, which is why I didn't bother her with my problems.

Mama asked me to make her another appointment with her doctor so maybe he could prescribe her some of those pills he gave Christian and Kory. Following her request, I called the doctor and they scheduled her appointment for one o'clock the upcoming Thursday.

I decided I would tell Daddy, even though Mama told me not to. Nor did she want anyone else to know. I know she still loves him and he *is* still her husband. Therefore, I felt he had a right to know what was going on with her health. I don't know what went wrong with them, and I still don't understand what made him cheat with a younger woman, but I hoped their marriage could survive the damage done.

I determined the best way to share with Daddy about how Mama had been feeling would be when he got home from work, instead of over the phone. He already knew she went to the doctor for yearly precautionary examinations since her mother and sister both died from cancer. However, she hid her recent tiredness from him.

About a month ago, she discovered a bump on the side of her neck right below her jawbone. When she first told me about it, I simply thought a bug might have bitten her, and I suggested she use the Benadryl ointment I've used on myself, Lance, and Alexis. I considered it the cure-all for most bites and rashes. After a few days of its use, Mama saw no improvement and started to worry the bump was more than a bug bite.

Whenever Mama got sick, she would get scared and fear the worst. She watched her mother and sister go from being healthy women, walking around causing hell, to women barely knowing their surroundings. That's the part Mama hated, watching them both in so much pain and suffering. Her biggest fear was that she, too, would be stricken with it.

I pray it's just stress and nothing else.

Chapter 34

Marcella

When I woke up, I had an eerie feeling about the day…something just didn't feel right to me. I'd been feeling real antsy lately, knowing any day the test results would arrive since six weeks had already passed. When the mailman came, I *really* got nervous.

Slowly, I opened the front door and reached inside the mailbox, pulling out a stack of mail. Just as I thought, the test results were back. I cursed the mailman for having placed the letter on top.

As I ripped open the envelope, I thought to myself that Lance was just going to have to be mad at me, because there was no way I was going to wait for him to get home to know the results.

The words stating there was a .001% chance that Lance Jap was the father of Selena Jap jumped out at me from the paper. I was both relieved and saddened. Relieved because it meant Lance wasn't Selena's father, but saddened because I'd grown to love her and looked forward to her visits. Lance wouldn't care one way or the other because he didn't have a relationship with her. It was just financial for Lance, but it was different for me. I cared for that child with every bone in my body, as if she was my own. It's her mama I couldn't stand. Before leaving to go down to Vyss, I decided to call Lance and inform him of the results.

What would become of Selena now?

Chapter 35

Karen

Christian informed me she was going to Washington DC to look for her mother. She told me after all that had happened to her over the past year, she couldn't continue not knowing if her mother was dead or alive. When the mayor told her he had some connections at the Department of Vital Statistics, Christian jumped at the opportunity to find Carmen.

Christian planned to leave in two days and asked me to go along with her, not wanting to go by herself. Since I didn't have a job or any other responsibilities, I agreed to go. She let me know upfront the whole process might take a couple of weeks, but she would cover all expenses. Hell, she didn't have to ask me twice. I was grabbing clothes out of my drawers before we hung up the phone.

I needed to get away. I couldn't remember the last time I left the city, and Davy was getting on my nerves calling my cell phone, leaving messages all day and night. His last message took the cake. He told me I had until the end of the week to come back home or else it was over. I thought I made it clear I wasn't coming back home and that the marriage was over when I moved all of my things out and moved back in with my parents two months ago. I just couldn't take the abuse and negative behavior. I wanted to call and leave him a message saying that by the end of the week, I would be in Washington DC with other things on my mind than coming back home to him. Instead, I left well enough alone and just erased the message, like I did the other fifty or so he had left prior.

When Kory dropped Christian and me off at the airport, I looked at my bags and then hers. She made me feel like I didn't own shit. Christian had Kory take *all* her bags out of the car. She had four suitcases, all Chanel of course, and there I stood with one suitcase and a bag I got on sale at Marshall's. I guess it was apparent I would be doing a lot of washing and re-wearing while we were gone.

With the flight being only an hour and a half, the pilot announced for us to prepare for landing before I could even get comfortable. Having never been to DC, I was excited, even though I knew we were there for business. Still, I was hoping we could visit some of the monuments since Christian had booked us a room at the Four Points on K Street, which was in the middle of downtown DC and a half mile from the White House.

Since it was after business hours on the first day we arrived, we did some sightseeing. We visited the outside of the White House and the Lincoln Memorial, and then we ended the day with a nice dinner at Morton's Steakhouse. We shared an appetizer of Jumbo Lump Crab Cake, and for my dinner, I had Cajun Ribeye Steak with steamed asparagus. Christian had the Baked Maine Lobster with an Idaho baked potato. We both had a glass of the house wine, with one glass leading to two and two leading to three, four, and five. By the time we finished, I was so drunk I could barely focus.

After finishing our food and countless glasses of wine, we walked back to the hotel. Upon entering the lobby, I overheard a couple talking about the live jazz band playing in the bar. I love jazz music. That's something Davy and I did have in common. I wanted to stop and listen to the band, but Christian said we needed to get plenty of sleep for the long day ahead of us tomorrow.

A good night's sleep is what I had indeed. Six-thirty the next morning, Christian tapped me on my shoulder to wake me. She wanted to be at the offices when they first opened, which would be around 8 or 8:30 a.m. And since we didn't know where the offices were located, she wanted us to leave out early so we would not waste any time.

After dressing, we took a cab to the Metropolitan Police Department on Indiana Avenue and spoke with Detective Arnold, who acted like he didn't have any information. At first, he was trying to bullshit us, but when Christian dropped Mayor Amir Dunkin's name, the detective was suddenly more than willing to help us out. He quickly placed a call to a woman by the name of Mrs. Walker at the National Center of Missing Adults in Phoenix, who said she would set us up with someone locally to help us out or point us in the right direction.

Twenty minutes later, Mrs. Walker called back with a contact name and an appointment time of 11:30 a.m. with the FBI. Christian wrote down all the information, thanked the detective, and then we left. Since it was only ten o'clock, we decided to go eat breakfast before heading over to 4th Street, which was right around the corner.

Right as we sat down to eat, Kory called and told Christian they'd received a letter about Amy, the teenager who had hit and killed KJ. At first, Christian didn't want to hear it, saying Amy had been mailing letters left and right trying to apologize. Kory said the one they received was different. It wasn't directly from her, but from the courts.

After excusing herself, Christian went in the lobby to talk to Kory in private. When she returned, her eyes were red and swollen. Just then, the waiter approached the table and I asked him to give us some additional time. We sat in silence while looking into each other's eyes. I didn't want to press Christian about the conversation. I knew if she wanted me to know, she'd let it out sooner or later.

"She's serving no time," Christian blurted out while breaking into an uncontrollable sob.

I sat in shock, choking on my orange juice. I couldn't believe what I had heard.

"She's getting off with a slap on the wrist of three years probation and having to do community service at the new football stadium."

I sat in disbelief. "Chris, she'll have to answer to a higher power than the judge. This always happens. When a white person does some shit, it's okay. If it had been a Shaniqua instead of an Amy, Shaniqua wouldn't see the light of day. She'd be in jail forever. This bitch hit my nephew and killed him, and she gets to work at the stadium and watch free games?! Where's the justice? Call Amir's ass!" I was so upset, I didn't want to eat.

"I refuse to call Amir. After all, he said he'd do what he could do. I guess he couldn't do much. Christian Banks doesn't beg anybody for anything. What I am going to do is call my attorney and request he file an appeal."

We ordered before Christian stepped back into the lobby to place her phone call.

After we ate breakfast at the Howard Johnson, HoJo as the locals called it, we headed for 4th street. We sat for two hours talking to an unattractive woman with pale white skin, bloodshot eyes, and a face that looked like someone hit her in it with a flat square pan. The stale smell attached to her body hit the air with her every movement. I could tell she had been in the business for a very long time because she was going from database to database with ease and telling us about cases she had worked in the past.

Christine informed Mary Lerner, the woman assisting us, how her aunt Whitney said Carmen was out in California the last time anyone had heard from her. Mary clicked onto another system and conducted a search for Carmen, but had no luck. Mary suggested we take a trip out to California and talk with the people there. She believed face to face contact produced better results. Christian expressed it wouldn't be a problem and that we could head out west the next day. She then asked Mary to set up the appointments and give us the contact names we would need to begin our search.

After Mary jotted down names and numbers on a piece of paper, she excused herself for about thirty minutes to make some calls. When she returned, she handed us all the information we would need. Upon leaving, we extended our hands for a shake and thanked her for all her help.

As soon as we returned to the hotel, Christian called Kory to check on Kamryn and to update him with everything that was going on. Kory must've thought we were on our way back home because I heard Christian tell him she was not returning home yet, but was headed to California instead. I assumed Kory was upset, because I then heard Christian tell him if he couldn't handle Kamryn to ask Marcella to watch her for a few days.

After ending her call with Kory, Christian grabbed the Yellow Pages and started calling the airlines. The first flight leaving out of DC the next day headed to LAX was at 9:15 a.m. Christian booked two reservations and then called the front desk to cancel the remaining nights and schedule for the shuttle to take us to the airport in the morning.

Since it was still early in the day, we headed out to window shop, and ended up in an urban wear store because Christian wanted to see if she could find something for Kory. I guess she figured a nice gift would keep him off her back. However, after looking up and down every aisle, she didn't buy anything. While she browsed, I sat by the door reading an urban magazine called *The Horizon*, a free publication. As I flipped through the magazine, I came across an advertisement for an agency searching for plus-size models. The company had two locations, one in New York and the other in Los Angeles, California. When we returned to the hotel, I immediately went to the Business Center to access the agency's website, telling Christian I would be up to the room shortly.

I figured since we would probably be in California for a few days, maybe I would have enough time to stop by the agency if it was located near where we would be staying. Everyone always said I have such a pretty face, and I felt a need to prove to Daddy and Davy that I was not a fuck up. Just because I was big didn't mean I wasn't beautiful.

Sunny California…that's the life I'm talking about. Christian stepped off the plane, looking like a movie star. She had her Chanel glasses on, her makeup looking all fresh. Not wanting to be outdone, I had Christian fix up my face while we were on the plane. As she was doing so, I shared with her that I had signed up with the modeling agency via email, and if we had time, I wanted to visit their office to see what they were about. Christian assured me we would find time to go to the agency. She even offered to do my hair and makeup for the appointment.

I don't have experience with modeling, but I know how to pull some shit off. Besides, I had a lot riding on this, so I had to make it work.

Chapter 36

Marcella

It was three o'clock, and Vyss was packed as it usually was on a Thursday afternoon. Everyone had clients in their chairs and a few under the dryers. I was on the phone taking an appointment and installing new software on the computer. I was also in the process of training the new receptionist, Jackie. I'd just finished typing the appointment in when this chickadee walked up to the counter. She was brown skin with a chin-length bob. It didn't look like her hair needed to be done, but her pimple-ridden face was another story. I was anxious to introduce her to a line of acne products Kory and Christian were selling. However, from the look on her bumpy face, I could tell she wasn't in the best of moods. So, I decided I would let her tell me her reason for coming in, as not to insult her.

"Hello, welcome to Vyss. My name is Marcella. How may I help you today?"

"I'm here to see Heather." She spoke straightforward and in a professional tone.

"Heather is with a client. Do you have an appointment?" I asked while scrolling down Heather's appointments for the day.

"Yes, I have a three-fifteen. I called the other day. It might have been you I talked to."

I didn't like the fact that she was insinuating I was the receptionist just because I was the one standing behind the desk at the time. But then again, how could she know differently if she was not a regular client.

"Okay, are you Nicole?" I asked with a smile on my face, trying to break the ice.

"Yes."

"Well then, I will let Heather know you're here. Please have a seat in the foyer to the left. Help yourself to coffee, tea, or a soft drink." I pointed in the direction of the waiting area and then called Heather to inform her that her next client had arrived. Heather informed me she would be finished with the client's head she was currently styling in about ten to fifteen minutes and to let Ms. Nicole Franklin know she'd be right with her.

When I went over to relay the message to *Ms. Franklin*, I overheard her on her cell phone arguing with someone, saying he had promised he'd leave his wife and now he was changing his mind. As if she felt me staring at her, Ms. Franklin looked up at me, rolling her eyes. Embarrassed by the fact that it may have seemed I was eavesdropping on her conversation, I mouthed to her that Heather would be with her in about fifteen minutes and quickly walked away.

Soon, Nicole was up pacing the floor, and then after a few more minutes of waiting, she came over and asked me when

Heather would be ready for her. I looked at the time and noticed Heather was over her fifteen minute time frame.

After five more minutes passed, Heather walked her former client to the receptionist area to cash out. As soon as her client had left, I reminded Heather of the fifteen-minute rule and let her know the fine would be deducted from her next paycheck, as well as papers would be written up for her to sign by the end of the day. Heather didn't say anything, but I could tell from her body language she was pissed. Oh well, her being mad was not my problem, but making sure that Vyss' reputation is upheld was.

Heather walked into the waiting area and sat down next to Nicole. She first apologized for her lateness, and then, while running her fingers through Nicole's hair, she informed her of all the services Vyss offered. As they proceeded to walk back to Heather's station, an uneasy feeling about Nicole overcame me.

As I stepped from behind the receptionist desk and headed to the back office, Kory stopped me and asked if I wanted something to eat because he was about to step out for a minute. Since it would soon be dinnertime, I ordered a Chicken Caesar Salad, handed Kory a ten-dollar bill, and then continued to the back.

After finishing my business in the office, I walked past Heather's station as she was putting a cape around Nicole's neck. I heard Heather calling in Tasha, her assistant, when Nicole started talking about knowing someone named Troy. Curious as to where Nicole was going with her statement, I posted myself outside of Heather's door to listen. Ignoring Nicole, Heather asked Tasha to wash her hair, deep condition it, and sit her under the dryer for ten minutes. That's when Nicole jumped in Heather's face and screamed that Troy was leaving her.

Nicole was all up in her face, forcing Heather to take a step back to put some distance between them. I leaned in closer to the doorway, wanting to hear everything Nicole was telling Heather, loud and clear, without being noticed.

"Just how do you know Troy, and what do you mean he's leaving me?" Heather asked, her voice rising.

Nicole went on to tell Heather how she met her husband at an after-work party downtown about six months ago, and how Troy told her black women didn't turn him on, but that there was something about her that sparked his interest.

"Bullshit!" Heather screamed. "Troy doesn't like black women. He's never liked black women. Now, please remove yourself from my chair. Tasha will see you out."

"Bitch, you're stupid! That's what's wrong with white women. They're stupid. You haven't noticed that Troy took up bowling on Thursday nights? The only pins he's knocking belong to me," Nicole spat, her hand upon her hip.

My body went numb and a cold chill ran through my body. I could only imagine what Heather was feeling. Next thing I knew, Heather swung on Nicole. Tasha, with her mouth gapping wide open, ran to the corner of the station to get out of the line of fire and yelled for someone to break it up. I, on the other hand, made no attempt to stop Heather, figuring I would have tried to kill the cunt if it were me in Heather's shoes.

I was front and center as people crowded outside of Heather's station to watch as she knocked the breath out of Nicole's ass. Nicole got enough strength to grab onto the chair and swing her leg around to kick Heather. That shit had to hurt, but Heather came back, knocking Nicole to the floor. It looked like Heather was going for broke. Everybody watched on in shock. I'm sure they figured the black bitch was going to kick Heather's white ass, but to everyone's surprise, that wasn't the case.

Heather kicked her repeatedly, trying her best to stomp Nicole's ass into the ground. Then, she leaned over and punched her dead in the face, smashing Nicole's broad nose. If Troy wanted Nicole, he'd get her when Heather was finished whooping her ass. Heather planned on mopping the floor with Nicole Franklin's ass for coming up to her job and embarrassing the hell out of her.

Heather was stomping and kicking her as hard as she could. With every word, she delivered a punch, a swing, or a kick. Heather then stared spitting in her face and dragging her by her hair out of her station. I guess she figured she needed more room to get at that ass the way she really wanted to. In a feeble attempt to escape Heather's grasp, Nicole bit her on the hand, breaking the skin, but that didn't stop Heather. By now, everyone in the shop was watching the catfight in progress.

Somehow, Nicole managed to get up from the floor and grabbed Heather's hair, pulling her down on the ground with her. Arms were flailing everywhere. Even though she was getting her ass beat, Nicole continued to talk shit.

As they rose to their feet, Nicole hollered about how she and Troy saw each other at least twice a week and that they had sex after their first date. She ended the shit by saying she was in love with Troy. With a force unknown, Heather slapped Nicole hard across the face, causing her to lose her balance and fall into a glass display. The whole display came crashing down, hitting a station in the process. Glass flew everywhere. Once Nicole got to her feet again, she picked up a piece of shattered glass and charged at Heather with it. Heather blocked her face, and as she did, Nicole sliced her arm wide open. The next thing I knew, Heather's hands were around her neck. I don't know if it was my imagination or what, but it looked like she was turning blue. At that very moment, I think she wanted to kill Nicole Franklin, and didn't give a fuck about the consequences.

Sharmaine and I jumped on Heather in an attempt to pry her hands from the cunt's neck. Heather released her grip, but they continued to go at it, though, throwing hits whenever they could. Sharmaine had Nicole, and Jacob and I held Heather while Maurice tried to put the display back up. I found out later it was his station the display had hit.

Making the mistake of thinking they had both calmed down to the point of being sensible, we released our holds on them. However, still enraged, Heather picked up a bottle of water and hit her in the face, then grabbed the shears from Angelique's station and stabbed Nicole in the shoulder.

As Anthony and Maurice grabbed Heather from behind, Nicole took advantage of the situation and hit Heather in the face with some flat irons. Breaking free of Anthony and Maurice's grip, Heather pounced on Nicole's ass once again and commenced to beating the daylights out of her. The shit was definitely out of control.

I knew everyone in the shop was surprised Heather could hang with that black cunt. I guess you could say they both had something in common regardless of their skin color, and that being, they both loved their black men.

Everyone who tried to break them up was pushed and knocked out of the way. It seemed as though Heather wasn't going to stop until she had killed the bitch. I don't know where she got the adrenaline rush, but she pushed Maurice out of the way and grabbed for Nicole's hair again. By this time, I knew they were getting tired by the way they both were panting and staggering about. It seemed like they'd been fighting forever, although I'm sure it had only been a few minutes.

Maurice was able to stop the fight for a second, but the big-mouth bitch still hadn't learned her lesson and continued to talk shit.

"I call your house and talk to your husband for hours while you're in the next room watching TV, you stupid heifer!" Nicole shouted while waving her hands in the air.

"Bitch, my husband doesn't have an interest in black women!" Heather retorted.

Nicole then grabbed Heather's shirt, ripping it off and screaming, "Once you go black, you never go back!"

Heather came right back at her with, "If it ain't white, it ain't right!"

It was time for round two, three, or whatever the fuck round they were on. Heather pushed Nicole against the receptionist stand and the monitor fell to the floor. I couldn't figure out why Nicole wouldn't give up, especially with the cut she had under her eye and the fucking stab wound to her arm.

Hoping my authoritative voice would put an end to the mayhem, I started yelling for them to stop. Not ready to give up just yet, Heather picked up a chair and threw it at Nicole, but her aim was off and the chair ended up crashing through the shop's front window.

The next thing I knew, the police were there to haul both of their asses off to jail. While one police officer positioned Heather in the backseat of the squad car, she watched with a pitiful look on her face as Maurice and I gave a statement to the other police officer.

As Kory approached the shop, he stopped in his tracks, dropped his bag on the sidewalk, and placed his hands over his face. While I explained to him what had happened, he looked at the squad car Nicole was in and then suddenly lunged in her direction, as if he were trying to get a hold of her. The police had to restrain him. He didn't even bother looking Heather's way.

I felt bad. I really did. I felt there was more I could've done to prevent all the damage to the shop, but everything had happened so fast.

Troy's car screeched to a stop in front of the shop, and he jumped out and started talking to Kory, who was walking around in circles.

"Man, this is definitely going to push my wife over the edge," is all I heard Kory say, which made me feel more like shit.

Just then, the officer got in his car, turned on the siren, and sped off. I assumed he was taking them to the nearest precinct.

Troy didn't even go over to the car to see if Heather was alright, the no-good dirty bastard. When Heather divorces his ass, she better forget all that shit about taking half. Hell, she better take it *all*.

Chapter 37

Marcella

With all the shit that had happened, I didn't feel like talking to anyone. A number I didn't recognize flashed on the caller ID of my cell phone. I bet whoever just called me was now ringing Kory's cell. He looked at the number and then cracked a "fuck you" smirk. Not saying anything, he threw the cell phone at me for me to check the number and see if it was the same bug-a-boo that had been calling my phone. And it most certainly was.

We both assumed it was someone trying to get the lowdown on what had transpired at the shop. I hoped that's what it was, and not Heather calling to get someone to post her bail. Don't get me wrong, I like Heather and all. I'm very appreciative of how she stepped in and helped my brother and sister-in-law keep from going under. And if a bitch came in the shop frontin' on me, I would've done the same damn thing. Right now, though, Heather would have to wait. Getting her ass out of jail was the last thing on my mind. I didn't *even* want to know what was going on in K-Boy's mind.

Needless to say, Kory sent all the workers home for the day. A few offered to stay behind to help clean up, but Kory refused their offer, letting everyone know the only one he wanted around to help him sort through the mess was me.

As I bent down to pick glass up off the floor, I heard the impact of something hitting the wall. Looking up, I saw Kory had thrown his cell phone. No damage was done, except for the battery popping off the back.

Just then, my phone started ringing again. Neither one of us wanted to answer because there was a possibility it could be Christian on the other end, and we weren't ready to explain anything to her. The next thing I knew, Kory had swept all the shit off of one employee's workstation onto the floor and grabbed my phone from out of my hand before I had a chance to look at the number.

Fear raced through my heart as Kory held the phone up to his ear in silence. I could hear the person on the other end talking, but I couldn't make out who it was or what they were saying. All of a sudden, Kory fell against the wall and dropped to his knees. I ran over, snatching the phone from him.

It was Daddy on the phone. He repeated to me that Mama had gone to the doctor about her exhaustion, and while checking her vitals, they discovered her blood pressure was low. He said she'd gone into cardiac arrest right there in the doctor's office.

I couldn't believe what I was hearing. I glanced over at Kory, who just sat with his back against the wall and an expressionless look on his face. No tears, no frown, no nothing. I felt lightheaded and had to lean against the wall to keep from falling.

Daddy told me he was at Providence Hospital, the same hospital that pulled the plug on my nephew. He said he was standing outside the emergency room and that Mama was going to be in surgery for the next few hours. I told him Kory and I would be at the hospital shortly. The last thing Daddy said before we hung up was to get Twin on the phone and tell her to get home.

Next, I called Tanisha to see if she could keep Kamryn and Alexis overnight, and she said it wouldn't be a problem. After I hung up the phone, tears started rolling down my face. Yes, Mama and I argued all the time, but she was still my mother and I didn't know what I would do if something happened to her. I'm a daddy's girl for sure, but there's no love like a mother's love.

I looked over at Kory, who still had a blank stare on his face. I knew if I was feeling fucked up, Kory had to be catching hell. His life had been turned upside down more than once over the last year.

The last time I was over at the house, I told Daddy about Mama's bump on her neck. He said he asked her about it, but she brushed him off, saying I had given her some ointment to apply to it. Now, I felt part to blame. I should've encouraged her to go see her doctor right away, instead of scolding her about always complaining about every little ache, pain, and bump. I didn't know it was that serious, or else I would've taken her to the doctor's myself.

I quickly dialed the number to call Lance and cried my way through the story about Mama. He asked where I was, and I informed him I was at the shop with Kory, then I briefly explained the chaos that had erupted at the shop earlier. Lance told me he would come to the shop immediately and drive us to the hospital.

I kept my eye on Kory, who had been sitting in silence ever since Daddy called. As I sat down at one of the stations, I thought of what to do next. *First thing, get Twin on the phone. Next thing, call the custodian to cleanup the place and put some boards up to the window where there was once glass. Third, get to the hospital in time to see Mama get out of surgery.*

While looking out the window, I spotted Lance pulling up, and ran outside to meet him. Lance looked in the shop from outside of the broken window. I knew what he was thinking…that the shop was fucked up. After entering the shop, he looked over at Kory, but didn't say a word.

Lance and I cleaned up as much as we could in the fifteen minutes it took Kevin and Louis to arrive. They came in and immediately got to work. Obviously, someone had called and informed them of what had happened earlier, and they'd been out getting things to shut down the shop temporarily. I wanted to hug them when they walked in. At least for the time being, I wouldn't have to worry about Vyss.

In a daze, Kory pulled his wallet out and tried to hand Louis everything in it. He was trying to pay them for a service he already had them on the payroll for. Louis took the money, but then handed it to me when Kory leaned his head back against the wall. I'd be sure to give it to Christian.

Oh shit! Christian! With everything going on, I had totally forgot to call her.

I called Karen's cell, but the voicemail kept picking up, so I tried Christian's phone and she answered on the first ring. When Kory, Lance, and I walked out to Lance's truck, I looked up and saw Selena asleep on Rosalita's lap in the back seat. *The nerve of him!* I didn't have time to question the shit, but I would be sure to address the situation later.

Upon arriving at the hospital, Kory refused to go in the room Mama was in. He said if something happened to Mama, he wanted to remember her the way he last saw her. I begged him to come in, but he kept refusing. So, Lance and I went in while Daddy stayed right outside the room with Kory, obviously understanding his unspoken pain.

Epilogue

Kory

It's been six months since my life was turned upside down once again. There has been a lot to be thankful for over these last few months. Christian and I are awaiting the trial date for the appeal we filed with our attorney. We are determined not to let the death of our son rest until justice is served, and we are willing to take it all the way to the Supreme Court, if need be.

Christian finally gave up filing for divorce. She said with all we've been through, there was no need to add more pain to our lives. We both promised to mend the issues we had and work on living our lives, while making sure Kamryn continued to receive the love and support she needed from both of her parents. I ain't gonna lie…it's been hard overlooking some of the sarcastic shit Christian says, but I'm in this marriage to stay, so I have no other choice.

Mama has gone through a lot, also. Her surgery was successful. They found out she had cancer, and now she's undergoing chemotherapy. Daddy goes to her appointments with her faithfully every Monday and Thursday. He actually took an early retirement so he could be home with Mama on a full-time basis. Ever since the onset of her illness, Mama is a changed person. She calls the house three or four times a week wanting Christian and Kamryn to come over and visit. I believe her reasons for focusing on Kamryn so much are to overcome the pain of not having KJ around and the scare of almost losing her life. I've heard death can either make you strong and mean or weak and nice. I guess Mama took on the weak and nice role. I kinda like the new Mama, but sometimes, I long to hear from the old Leslie Banks, always fussing, cussing, and in everybody's business.

Twin…I mean, Karen…has it going on. Hell, she may be on the road to big-time stardom. Karen got a call from a modeling agency in New York about three months ago. She wasn't able to make the appointment she had when her and Christian was in L.A., but not to be discouraged, she sent them some headshots a couple of weeks after she returned home. Shortly after receiving the photos, the modeling agency paid for her to fly out so they could talk with her about the possibility of her modeling for them. Next thing I knew, Karen came back home and called a family meeting with me, Marcella, Mama, Daddy, Christian, and Davy. She announced she was moving to New York within the next couple of weeks to become a plus-size model and that she had already signed a one-year contract.

The news threw me off. I mean, Karen does have a pretty ass face, but I never pictured her as a model. I got to give it to Twin. She has really come out of her shell over the last couple of years. I almost shit my pants when, at the end of the family meeting, Karen announced in front of everyone that she also filed for divorce from Davy. His ass sat there with the dumbest look on his face. I'm sure he was thinking about all those big dollars he would be missing out on. He doesn't deserve her anyway. I knew he hadn't been doing her right. Even though Twin would never admit it, I knew he was kicking her ass. I know when someone is trying to cover up a black eye with concealer. Davy was so embarrassed he left without saying one word, slamming the front door behind him.

Marcella is so deep in love that she can't see her husband is playing the shit out of her. I still need to confront that nigga Lance regarding the stunt he pulled that day at the shop when he had his "so-called" baby mama and daughter in the truck when he came to pick us up. I was too fucked up to say shit at the time, and I haven't seen his ass since then, but I got some words for him.

I asked Marcella what the fuck was up with Lance, and she came up with some bullshit ass story, telling me how when he was on his way to pick us up, he saw Rosalita and Selena at the bus stop. He told her he offered them a ride home, but didn't have time to drop them off before coming to Vyss to take us to the hospital.

That shit doesn't make any sense to me. Marcella told me the little girl wasn't even his, so why does he feel the need to play Good Samaritan? She needs to tell that nigga to leave the past in the past. When the test results came back saying he wasn't the father, he should have stepped right then. In my opinion, I think they're still fucking around. Lance is another no-good nigga that doesn't deserve her. She should divorce his ass and take him for child support and alimony, which would serve his ass right for fucking over my lil' sister.

But who am I? Different strokes for different folks. I guess some of us just like living… *Dangerously.*

XpressYourself Novels

QTY

____ *Anything Goes* by Jessica Tilles ISBN: 0-9722990-0-9
____ *In My Sisters' Corner* by Jessica Tilles ISBN: 0-9722990-1-7
____ *Apple Tree* by Jessica Tilles ISBN: 0-9722990-2-5
____ *Sweet Revenge* by Jessica Tilles ISBN: 0-9722990-3-3
____ *One Love* by Bill Holmes ISBN: 0-9722990-4-1
____ *Fatal Desire* by Jessica Tilles ISBN: 0-9722990-4-1
____ *Dangerously* by Makenzi ISBN: 0-9722990-7-6

Send to:
Xpress Yourself Publishing, LLC
Attn: Book Orders
P.O. Box 1615
Upper Marlboro, MD 20773

Please send me the books I have checked above. I am enclosing $_____ ($15.00/book plus $2.00 per book, shipping and handling). Send check or money order (no cash or C.O.Ds please). Allow up to two weeks for delivery.

Name _____

Address _____

City _____State/Zip _____

Visit us online at www.xpressyourselfpublishing.org

Printed in the United States
72326LV00008B/61-72